Praise for Heather MacAllister

"Heather MacAllister does a masterful job in this perfectly crafted, compact romance that gets better with every page."
—*Affaire de Coeur* on *Kept in the Dark*

"This is a fun, fast-paced read that I was sad to see come to an end."
—*Goodreads* on *A Man for All Seasons*

"Lovely, witty dialogue and believable characters."
—*The Good, The Bad, and The Unread* on *His Little Black Book*

"Pure fantasy in the finest sense, Heather MacAllister's *Never Say Never* crackles with sexy banter."
—*RT Book Reviews*

"Smart and sassy, Heather MacAllister's *Tempted in Texas* is highlighted by strong characterizations and witty dialogue."
—*RT Book Reviews*

"A one-sitting read for me. I got so caught up in this story that I really didn't want it to end."
—*The Best Reviews* on *Male Call*

Blaze

Dear Reader,

I got the idea for *Tall, Dark and Reckless* after following an endless path of suggested internet links while researching a different book. There's so much advice on how to attract/keep/entertain/feed/train/meet men—and it was all different. Then I landed on one site that promised to cut through all the babble and simply list the traits and qualities of the perfect man. As a bonus, it listed the instant deal breakers.

Now, you know where I'm going with this. Their deal breakers weren't my deal breakers. And to be honest, when I found my perfect man, even my original deal breakers turned out not to be deal breakers. Perfect doesn't mean flawless, it means perfect for me. This is exactly what Piper Scott learns when she discovers that tall, dark and reckless Mark Banning is her perfect man. I hope you enjoy watching her figure it out.

Best wishes,

Heather MacAllister

www.HeatherMacAllister.com
http://www.facebook.com/HeatherMacAllisterBooks
https://twitter.com/#!/Heather_Mac

Heather MacAllister

TALL, DARK & RECKLESS

HARLEQUIN®
entertain, enrich, inspire™

Recycling programs
for this product may
not exist in your area.

ISBN-13: 978-0-373-79699-1

TALL, DARK & RECKLESS

Copyright © 2012 by Heather W. MacAllister

ABOUT THE AUTHOR

Heather MacAllister lives near the Texas gulf coast where, in spite of the ten-month growing season and plenty of humidity, she can't grow plants. Heather has written more than forty-five romance novels, which have been translated into 26 languages and published in dozens of countries. She's won a Romance Writers of America Golden Heart Award, *RT Book Reviews* awards for best Harlequin Romance and best Harlequin Temptation, and is a three-time Romance Writers of America RITA® Award finalist. When she's not writing stories about where life has its quirks, Heather collects vintage costume jewelry, loves fireworks displays, computers that behave, and sons who answer their mother's texts. You can read her posts at www.BlazeAuthors.com/blog or visit her at www.HeatherMacAllister.com, like her on www.facebook.com/HeatherMacAllisterBooks, or follow her at https://twitter.com/#!/Heather_Mac.

Books by Heather MacAllister

HARLEQUIN BLAZE

To get the inside scoop on Harlequin Blaze and its talented writers, be sure to check out blazeauthors.com.

To the Fishinglights gang:
Mike and Rae, John and Linda, and Stuart.

And in memory of Kathy.

Prologue

1

Step one: Find a perfect man.

ORDINARILY, PIPER SCOTT wouldn't be distracted by a pair of blue eyes, no matter how attractively they crinkled, or a strong, manly jaw, no matter how chiseled—except these eyes were squinting and the jaw was definitely gritting. In pain.

Moments earlier, Piper had arrived at the entrance to the offices of OMG, the Online Media Group, at the same time as the owner of the crinkly blue eyes and the chiseled jaw.

"I'll get it," he'd said, and leaned around her to open the front door.

"Thanks," she'd replied, because her cell had just buzzed and at that moment she was grabbing at her purse to check the caller ID. Only then her purse had slipped down her arm and tangled with the strap of the tote bag she carried on the same arm. When she'd heaved them back in place, a jacket in the dry cleaner's bag slung over her other shoulder had slithered off its hanger and fallen to the leaf-strewn concrete in front of the door. As she bent to retrieve the jacket, the tote bag fell forward and made contact with the leg of the owner of the blue eyes and chiseled jaw.

Slight contact. A little bump. And now he was acting as though she'd bashed him with a load of books or something.

The big baby.

She'd automatically apologized, one of those quick, social "I'm sorrys" that didn't seem adequate in the face of that grimace.

"I'm really sorry," she added now.

"It's okay." He gave her a game smile.

Piper eyed him, trying to read his expression. Was she missing something? She glanced down and discovered his hand clenched around his thigh.

White knuckles, expensive jeans. The jeans had the careful whiskering that always reminded Piper of those lines in the comic books meant to emphasize something. "Look! Wow!" In this case, it was the crotch area, which, she noted, did not need emphasizing.

When Piper became aware that she was standing on a public street in downtown Austin eyeing a stranger's crotch—truly not like her—she jerked her eyes upward. "I didn't realize I hit you that hard. There's not that much in my bag."

"You didn't." He straightened. Somewhat. "Something hard got me in the right—or wrong—place."

"I don't have— Oh. It must have been the flatiron."

He looked questioningly.

"A hair styling thingie."

"Ah." He raised his hand and went for the door again.

Piper heard the tiny, hard breath he sucked between his teeth.

Oh, please. He was being so transparent. She knew what was coming next. He'd hit on her. So to speak. Anyway, they'd walk in together and she'd apologize again because he was so *obviously* suffering and then he'd say, "If you really want to make it up to me, have coffee with me." Or "Let me buy you a drink." Or even "You can buy me a drink." Probably not "You can kiss it and make it better," a line mostly used by guys who weren't as good-looking. And only the ones who hadn't been pepper sprayed after saying it.

As they walked across the foyer's hardwood floor, Piper waited for him to make his move. He'd better hurry. The foyer wasn't that big. It didn't need to be, since OMG only published digitally and the writers were scattered all over the country. Even Piper didn't come here all that often and she lived nearby.

The headquarters of the online conglomerate was in a small, former residential dorm near the University of Texas campus and still had the living/dining/kitchen layout, which OMG used as the downstairs conference space. The offices were upstairs.

The area downstairs was empty now, but in less than half an hour, the OMG quarterly meeting would begin and Piper would be sitting at the table providing support to Dancie, her former college roommate and technically her OMG boss, but first and foremost her friend. Her best friend. The friend who'd been there when Piper needed a friend. Now Dancie needed her, even if she wouldn't admit it.

But in the meantime, Mr. Blue Eyes was limping. *Limping.* Fine. Might as well get this over with and let him down easy.

Pasting on a semi-smile, Piper looked toward the man at her side. Only he wasn't at her side. He, without a backward look, flirtatious or otherwise, was making his way to the elevator.

She hesitated, one foot on the steps, and watched as he reached for the call button. Then he waited, not even glancing over to see if she was still there.

So…he wasn't going to hit on her? Well, that was lowering. Or, worse, was he *avoiding* her because he thought she was going to hit—metaphorically this time—on *him?*

Piper honestly didn't know and that was rare, because Piper knew men. Everything about them. It was her business to know. As Piper Scott, The Dating Doc, she'd counseled countless men and women—mostly women—on dating strategies. She was known for her exit interviews, a frank discussion of why the date hadn't worked. After interviewing a thousand men—actually, a thousand and thirteen men—she'd written *The Piper Plan: How to Land Your Perfect Man*.

Unfortunately, after interviewing those thousand men, Piper felt that there was nothing more to learn about the human male. Men had ceased to surprise her. They bored her.

Take the blue-eyed limper: he was the kind of handsome that appealed to women of all ages. He had arresting good looks—a shock of black hair and heavy black brows that contrasted with brilliantly blue eyes. She assumed he had a great smile, although she hadn't seen much of it. He even looked vaguely familiar, but most men did these days.

The point was, she knew his type, grid square alpha-alpha, the confident, popular, leader type, normally not a type attracted to her.

And clearly not this time, either. She was surprised to feel a flicker of disappointment.

Piper noticed that he'd pressed the button for the basement, which meant he was going to the man cave where the *Guys of Texas* webzine, helmed by her friend Dancie's twin, Travis, had its office. He was probably a friend of Travis's. They were the same confident, good-looking, women-magnet type of male.

But using the elevator for one flight down? Piper climbed the stairs wondering if the limp had been genuine after all, since it clearly wasn't a ploy to gain her sympathy prior to asking her out. Or maybe he *was* avoiding her. Or married. Or…whatever.

What really concerned her was that she didn't know. What a horrible time to lose her touch at sizing up men. She needed to be confident going into today's meeting.

Because this, *this* was the meeting where Dancie should

be named an equal partner with her father and brother—something that should have been done in the beginning.

And Piper was going to do everything in her power to make it happen.

Then, she and Dancie would be even.

MARK COULD HEAR THE CABLES and machinery as the tiny elevator moved in the shaft.

Hurry. His leg throbbed and he was aware that he hadn't heard the woman's footsteps continue up the stairs.

Yeah, he'd overdone the physical therapy yesterday, but he'd wanted to prove to Travis—and himself—that he was a hundred percent. The last thing he needed was to draw attention to his leg.

She was watching him so he knew he hadn't covered his pain as effectively as he'd hoped. The fact that she'd arrived in time for the meeting meant she probably wrote for OMG, too. Probably for Travis's sister, since she was headed upstairs.

Hurry, he urged the elevator again as cogs chugged and drew the box from whatever floor it had been parked at. He shifted all his weight off his leg, preparing to lurch inside as soon as the doors opened.

Go upstairs, he mentally urged the woman. She'd probably recognized him and that was why she was hesitating. Maybe she was a fan. Or, please no, a student in one of his journalism classes, the one in the lecture hall. Maybe she was about to approach him and try to carry on a conversation. Sweat beaded his upper lip and he knew from hours staring at himself in the mirrored walls of the Austin Physical Therapy Center that his face was a grayish-green. That gray-green color told him he was pushing himself to his limit and beyond. If he wasn't gray with pain, he wasn't working hard enough.

But a different set of muscles were screaming this time. Had she dislocated his knee or something when she'd hit him?

Something. Definitely something. The elevator arrived.

Mark forced himself to step forward as though nothing was wrong and propelled his body to the back of the tiny compartment where he grabbed on to the bar. His leg quivered and nearly buckled.

He suspected he was going to have to take a pain pill, something he'd wanted to avoid. He needed a clear head for this meeting. Not only did he have to demonstrate that he was ready to return to the field, he had to convince Travis's father to send him back to the Texas-Mexico border. Maybe not as his first assignment after his involuntary layoff, but soon. He had a story to finish and a smuggler to expose. And a promise to be kept.

The elevator doors shuddered closed and Mark gingerly explored the area above his knee, his fingers finding the depression where he'd lost a hunk of muscle and flesh. No, he wouldn't be playing a game of three-man basketball anytime soon.

On the slow descent, the pain receded, at least enough for Mark to limp into the *Guys of Texas* man cave.

There were usually a half dozen or so guys hanging around, thinkin' about guy stuff. Doin' guy stuff. Writing about guy stuff. Thinkin' about women from a guy's point of view: how to get them and what to do with them when you get them, how long and how many times you could do it, and any tips and tricks to share with fellow guys so you could keep doing it.

It would drive him nuts if he had to do that every day, but it was obviously popular. Travis Pollard had turned a simple online campus blog into a megamoneymaker for OMG.

The *Guys of Texas* published Mark's behind-the-scenes commentary as he researched in-depth foreign exposés for the news division of OMG. His column was all about the glamour. The adventure. The danger. The excitement. The women.

Yes, Mark was Fantasy Guy. He exhaled. At least it paid the bills.

Mark hung his jacket on a set of longhorns and headed toward the coffee bar.

"Mark!" Travis jogged toward him and Mark realized he'd thought Mark might not show today. "Marko!"

Travis knuckle-bumped him. "My man! *The* man. Über-guy—"

"Travis."

Travis stuck his hand into his pocket. "Glad you're back."

"I got that."

"*Really* glad you're back."

"I got that, too."

"Yeah." Travis rubbed at the top of his nose. "Missed your columns these last couple of quarters. Teaching college courses and recovering from a gunshot wound isn't as popular as actually *getting* shot."

Mark studied the fancy machine at the coffee bar. It was new. "I was also stabbed—maybe you shouldn't have edited that out."

"Hey, man. It was in the same leg. Nobody would have believed it." Travis was completely serious. "But you're back now," Travis said as Mark pushed a combination of buttons that yielded a small cup of very black coffee with a thin layer of tan foam. "My sister has been kicking my behind in revenue."

"What's she got?"

Travis waved him to a chair. "A dating columnist. You know how women are. So right now, she's got a lot of women running up the page stats. But when you're on your game, we get the guys *and* the gals." Travis mock-punched Mark in the jaw. "Good thing they cut your leg and not your face."

Mark gazed at him, his expression carefully blank.

"'Cause that face is your meal ticket," Travis continued.

"Because talent counts for nothing, right?" Mark asked.

"No, because there are a lot of talented people and there are a lot of good-looking people. There are even a lot of tal-

ented, good-looking people. But there aren't a lot of lookers
who are willing to work it. They don't have to. You work it.
I don't know what drives you and I don't want to know. I'm
just glad you do what you do."

Travis was no slouch in the work/talent/looks department,
either. However, he hadn't made eye contact very often during
their conversation—which had been more Travis rambling
than a conversation. And now, he'd started bouncing a tennis
ball against the wall, repeatedly hitting the same smudged
spot. Mark had interviewed enough people to know Travis
was holding something back, and that something was going
to affect Mark and his return to work.

"What aren't you telling me?" he asked.

Travis stopped bouncing the ball and gazed directly at
Mark. "Dancie's *Women's Guide* numbers are better than the
Guys of Texas, even with you. Maybe not you being rescued
after being captured, but better than normal you."

All Mark wanted was to get back to normal. Normal was
following his subject for days on end, immersing himself in
whatever culture he found himself. Normal was not facing
hundreds of starry-eyed journalism students three times a
week. Normal was not evaluating every conversation and
every word of every conversation with dozens of beautiful
young women lest he inadvertently encourage romantic fan-
tasies. Okay, maybe there was a little normal there. "So your
sister has found something as popular as my column. How
exactly am I supposed to take that?"

"You aren't. That's why I wasn't telling you, but you
asked."

"It's what I do."

"And I hope you'll be doing it for a long time."

"So do I." There was still an undercurrent of tension in
the conversation.

Travis cleared his throat and shifted. "And you shouldn't
worry about today's quarterly."

Mark hadn't. Until now.

"I just thought it wouldn't hurt to have you here in person to remind my dad of how much of an asset you are."

"So it isn't usual for a contributor to come to these meetings."

"Well, I mean, writers do sometimes." Travis shifted again and finally got to his feet and walked to the ordinary drip coffeemaker next to the fancy machine. "Like if they're new and going to be major or there's going to be changes. Coffee?" He held up the pot after mumbling the last.

Mark shook his head. "Changes that concern me?"

Travis poured two mugs anyway. "I don't know, and that's the truth. It depends on Dancie. She's kinda in the driver's seat for the first time and, to be honest, I don't know what kind of a driver she is."

Travis had asked Mark to be here today. Maybe his sister had asked her heavy hitter to be here, as well. Mark's mind flickered back to the woman he'd opened the door for. He tried to recall details of her appearance, but basically retained only an impression of glasses, brownish-blondish hair and a bunch of straps. He'd been distracted by the sudden pain in his leg and what it meant and how, or if, he'd be able to conceal it. He hadn't been paying attention to her, other than getting the impression that while she was young, she wasn't as young as the females in the journalism classes he taught. "Your sister's big gun…"

"Piper Scott?"

"Um, I don't know."

"I guess I can't expect you to read the competition." Travis handed him a mug. "The Dating Doc."

Mark shook his head.

"She's a dating coach. She's got some theory about men and their dating personalities that has just taken off."

"Do you think she'll be here today?"

Travis sipped his coffee. "If Dancie's smart, she will. Piper lives here in Austin. They used to be roommates."

Mark had a feeling. "What's she look like?"

"Normal pretty—not the high-maintenance kind. Medium tall, good body, but she doesn't show it off."

Mark tried to remember the woman at the door, but mostly he remembered her voice. Politely sympathetic with an attractive huskiness. Yeah, he liked her voice, now that he thought about it.

"She's kind of reserved." Travis gave a half smile. "Not the party-girl type. The type you'd want to be your sister's roommate."

"Gotcha. I think I saw her as I came in."

"You probably did." Travis hitched his hip onto the corner of his desk. "Here's the thing. With you on the sidelines, Dancie's division has been bringing in the most money and she's going to make a play for being named partner."

Mark didn't like the implication. Actually, it wasn't an implication. Travis was coming right out and saying that his division had lost ad revenue because Mark hadn't been on assignment since late last year. Travis would be pushing for his return. Good to know.

Travis sipped his coffee, and Mark did the same. Pretty good coffee. It might even be better than the coffee from the fancy machine.

"Doesn't your sister deserve to be a partner?" Mark wondered why she hadn't been from the beginning, but that wasn't his business.

"She might at this point in time. But she's going to get married eventually. And then she'll have babies and she'll slack off and still get one-third of the profits. Dad will go gaga over the grandkids and *he'll* slack off and I'll be doing all the work for one-third of the money."

Mark grimaced. "Isn't that view kind of…"

"Retro?" Travis supplied.

"Not the word I would have used, but yes."

"Hang political correctness. It's the truth." Travis stopped short of slamming his mug on the desk, but he set it down heavily. "Look, Dancie and I had a great childhood. I know people call my mom a trophy wife. So what? Sure, she's blonde and a lot younger than my dad, but she's not stupid. And she was there for us and my dad. When I'm lucky enough to have kids, I want to be able to give them a full-time mom, too. And I know Dancie isn't going to let someone else raise her kids if she doesn't have to."

Mark stared unblinkingly. "Some mothers don't have that luxury."

Travis caught himself. "Hey, man. I forgot about your mom being in the military. I'm sure she did the best she could."

Mark clenched his fist so hard he almost forgot about the pain in his leg. "So your point is that your sister shouldn't be a partner because she might have children?"

"My point is that I want to avoid doing a lot more work for a lot less money. You heard the one-third money part, right? That means the *Guys of Texas* will have less operating funds. That means less money for your expensive little adventures, as popular as they are."

This time when Mark sipped his coffee, he burned his tongue, which was good because otherwise he'd be using it to tell Travis to go to hell. On his "little adventures," Mark rooted out corruption, fighting against rulers and thugs who terrorized their citizens as they made power grabs. He exposed tribal chiefs and gang leaders who showed gratitude to the foreign-aid folks while they took the money for their own use. Because of Mark's "little adventures," people's lives had been saved. Wars had been stopped. Leaders deposed. Mark reported the stories, but the behind-the-scenes "little adventures" were what Travis printed as columns in the *Guys of Texas* webzine. Mark didn't like the trivialization, but the advertising revenue was what got him overseas.

He'd had offers from more prestigious news services, but he'd always been a loner and he liked the freedom OMG gave him. He didn't have to answer to a news team or a producer, except Travis and Travis's father, and as long as Mark got the story, he could do what he wanted, how he wanted.

Sure, they yelped a couple of times and sure, Mark skated in the gray area, but he got stories the larger media services could only dream about.

"So," Travis continued. "We want to do whatever it takes to get you back in the field."

On this, they could agree. "The PT is going great." Mark ignored the throbbing in his thigh. "By the end of the semester I'll be good to go." It was late October. His leg had another couple of months to heal. Plenty of time.

"Great." Travis clapped his hands together before pointing them at Mark. "Let's talk possible assignments."

Mark met his eyes with the same gaze that had compelled everyone from beggars to royalty to tell him more than they'd meant to. "I've been gone so long, I want to make a splash with my comeback."

"Keep talking."

"Burayd al-Munzir." Mark sat back.

Travis gazed unblinkingly. "And he is…?"

How could he not know? Swallowing his irritation, Mark said, "Fatik al-Munzir's youngest half brother. Burayd's mother came from an influential tribal family in El Bahar, and they were not pleased when she became a third wife instead of the first wife as arranged. His mother's people are backing Burayd in a disagreement with Fatik over who has rights to the mega oil reserves sitting under tribal lands. Each side wants to be the one to parlay with the U.S., but nobody in this country is taking Burayd seriously. And they need to. The story will take months to develop, but it'll be worth it." And staying in villas in modern cities would be easier on his leg than hiking around mountains.

"Sounds very promising," Travis said. "But we need something with a faster payoff."

Mark gritted his teeth. "Some issues are more important than money."

"I like that you think that way and I don't ever want you to be in a position to realize how wrong you are." Travis stopped, met his eyes and gave Mark a big, fat smile. "But money is what will buy the plane ticket to get you to whatever sandbox these two play in. Money is what rescued you the last time you went rogue. And money is what has paid for all your physical therapy sessions."

"Yeah." Mark shifted as his leg twinged. Keeping his tone offhand, he said, "So how about I go back to the border and finish the gun smuggling story?"

"You've gotta be kidding."

"It could be a fast turnaround. I've already done the research—"

"No." Travis spoke with unmistakable finality. "Not now. Not ever. At least, not if you want to continue writing for OMG."

Mark wasn't a total idealist, but he'd never sold out and he never would. He tamped down his anger. "Are you threatening me?"

"Do facts threaten you? It was an expensive mistake."

"Is there a problem, Travis?" This was the first time Travis had ever mentioned money in considering Mark's assignments.

"Not at the moment, but the more slices, the smaller the piece of pie."

His sister's success must have really rattled Travis. "Have you considered that maybe Dancie will make it a bigger pie?"

"Like I said—marriage, babies." Travis was sounding a lot like his father. Mark had always thought it was an act, but maybe not.

"This is temporary for her," Travis reiterated. "I don't mind giving her a salary bump. I don't even mind if she draws a bigger salary than I do. But a partner's share of the profits? No."

Mark had no intention of getting in the middle of a family fight. He'd keep his thoughts to himself and by New Year's, he'd be on a plane to the Middle East. Or taking care of unfinished business at the border.

Travis checked his clunky gold watch and indicated that it was time to leave. "Bring all the enthusiasm you've got to the meeting, but don't forget to tie any story ideas to potential revenue streams for OMG."

Was Travis always like this before meeting with his father? If so, Mark was glad he'd never before attended one of these quarterly get-togethers.

Mark tried not to limp as they walked to the elevator. Potential revenue streams? That wasn't his job. His job was to get the story. Their job was to publish it.

For a moment Mark imagined a world in which he would never "adventure" again. He did not want to be a part of that world. Even so, though he might be forced to compromise, he'd never sell out.

2

Step two: Verify your target male's type. Only then engage him in light conversation.

AFTER REALIZING THAT THE MAN wasn't going to turn around, Piper had quietly continued up the stairs, so he wouldn't hear her and think she'd been standing there watching him. Of course, she had been, but she definitely didn't want him thinking so.

Her phone buzzed again as she reached the top of the steps and once again, she sent it to voice mail. Then she turned to the right and breezed into Dancie's office.

Startled, Dancie looked up from her computer. "You're way early!"

"Good morning!" Piper sang.

Dancie brightened. "Did you bring coffee?"

"Couldn't carry it." Piper set her bag and the hanging clothes on the one visitor's chair in the tiny space.

"Well, darn." Dancie went back to typing. "Travis took the good coffeepot and I don't feel like braving the man cave this morning."

Someone might have made coffee in the downstairs kitchen for the meeting. As Piper considered whether to check and possibly snag a cup for Dancie, her phone went off again. This time, she just let it buzz until it rolled over to voice mail on its own.

Forget the coffee. There wasn't that much time before the meeting started and Dancie needed the makeover fairy to wave her magic wand. Piper didn't have a magic wand, but she did have a flatiron, makeup and a change of clothes. Gently, she closed the door. "Are those notes for today, or can you take a break?"

Dancie stopped typing and eyed Piper suspiciously. "Why?" Her gaze drifted to the chair and narrowed.

Long ago, Piper had learned that the way to manipulate Dancie was to keep her off balance by moving quickly and decisively. Talking a lot as she did so helped, too.

"I want to tweak your visual presentation." As she spoke, Piper walked around Dancie's desk and pulled her out of the chair.

"What do you mean?"

There was a full-length mirror on the door. Piper positioned Dancie in front of it and tugged the faded navy hoodie off her arms.

"What are you doing?" Dancie jerked at a sleeve.

"Honestly, Dancie!" Piper pointed to a hole where the cuff had pulled away from the rest of the sleeve.

"Nobody's going to notice that!"

Piper freed the hoodie from Dancie's clutches and tossed it onto the desk. She should have aimed for the trash basket. "Only because you're dressing to be invisible."

"What are you talking about?" Dancie gestured down at her cotton tank, jean shorts, and flip-flops. "This is the way I always look! Everybody in Austin looks this way!"

"Not today." Piper examined Dancie's legs. At least she'd shaved them relatively recently. "Today, you're going to look like a partner in the Online Media Group."

Dancie went still. Anticipating the coming rant, Piper used the opportunity to remove the plastic bag from the clothes.

And then, the rant began. "If Dad makes me a partner like Travis, it's going to be because the *Women's Guide to Living Fabulous* division has brought in the most revenue the past two quarters and not because of what I'm wearing!"

"Of course it will be." Piper automatically spoke with the same tone she used to deliver unpleasant truths to defensive clients. "If he listens to you."

"That's why I have a written report. It's with our proposal." Dancie pointed to the desk where a shiny red folder sat. "Hard copy."

"Red. I see." At least Dancie'd put the thing in a folder.

"Yeah. I thought it would stand out."

"It does. Red means stop. Danger. Red ink. In the red." From the bag on the chair, Piper withdrew a green folder and handed it to Dancie. "Green is the color of money. It means growth. Go. Green is good." Piper gestured. "Switch the folders."

Dancie stared at it. "You actually brought a folder for me?"

"I didn't want you to stress in case you forgot."

Dancie walked toward the desk. "This is some of your psychological stuff, isn't it?"

"Yes." While Dancie changed her report folder, Piper moved the chair in front of the mirror.

Without turning around, Dancie said, "I see the clothes. Don't think I'm not aware of what you're doing. You're going to say, 'Dancie, your quarterly report says the same thing. You've just changed the cover to make it more appealing. That's all we're doing with these clothes. You're still you— you'll just have a different cover.'"

"Excellent. We can skip that part, then." Piper held up a skirt. "And one of the advantages of having roomed with you is that I know your size."

Dancie saw the skirt. "Oh, hell, no."

"Watch the potty mouth. Your dad doesn't like it when women swear."

"I am *not* wearing a skirt! I do not wear skirts. I have never worn skirts—something you should have picked up on after three years of rooming with me."

"It's a denim pencil skirt." Piper tossed it at her. "Think of it as a pair of shorts with the legs sewn together."

"He'll know I'm wearing it just to get on his good side."

"There's nothing wrong with your father seeing you make an effort to look more attractive," Piper said calmly. "You're trying to woo him—"

Dancie flung down the skirt. "In the first place, I am not one of your dating clients and in the second, ew!" She shuddered. "Gee, thanks for putting that in my head!"

"Compatibility principles are the same whether you're talking dating or job interviews or roommate questionnaires." The meeting was less than twenty minutes away now and Dancie was being more hardheaded than Piper expected. "Salesmen use the technique all the time. And that's what you are today—a salesman. You are selling yourself as a partner to your father."

"Ew—ew—ew—ew!"

"Dancie, stop it!" Piper had to speak more sharply than she wanted to, but this was important.

"Travis doesn't have to do stuff like this!" Dancie wailed.

"But he does." Piper looked around for an outlet to plug in the flatiron and ended up unplugging Dancie's desk lamp. "Have you seen Travis today? What's he wearing?"

Dancie made a disgusted sound. "Khaki Dockers and a UT golf shirt."

"And probably his big gold fraternity ring. What do you think your dad's going to wear?"

"What he always wears," Dancie said. "Dockers with his belly hanging over the waist and a golf shirt with a Longhorn football booster logo…" She met Piper's eyes as she trailed off.

"Exactly. Travis mirrors your father."

"Then I'll wear khakis and a golf shirt!"

"Your father likes pretty, feminine women." Which was why Piper was rocking a retro sorority girl/receptionist look today.

"Oh, I know," Dancie snapped. "He wants nothing more than for me to be his little princess until he can hand me off to Prince Charming."

"So be a princess with a brain." Piper led Dancie to the chair in front of the mirror and pushed on her shoulders. Unresisting, Dancie sat down, staring unseeingly until she noticed Piper with the flatiron in the reflection.

"Are you cra—"

Piper moved fast, grabbing a hank of Dancie's curly ponytail and running the iron through it.

Dancie jerked away in outrage. "Look what you've done! Now part of my hair is straight and part is curly!"

"Oops," Piper said, not sorry at all. "I guess I'll just have to straighten the rest of it, then."

Glaring, Dancie yanked the elastic off her ponytail. "I'm going to look pathetic!"

"No—"

"Yes, I am! There's nothing you can do to me that will make me look one-tenth as good as my mother looks when she rolls out of bed in the morning! You making me look all girlie is only going to emphasize it."

Her beauty queen mother was Dancie's huge hot button and there was no way around it. Better that she vent now than lose her cool during the meeting.

"Travis is the one who looks like Mom!" Dancie said of her twin.

True. Piper stayed silent and kept flat-ironing Dancie's frizzy hair. If Dancie would use some product, she'd have great waves. But she didn't, so Piper was going for long, loose and feminine today.

"He got the blond hair and the blue eyes and the great teeth and the dimple. I ended up with Dad's brown eyes and kinky black hair and mustache. I got mom's nose, though," Dancie continued bitterly. "It was a gift for my sixteenth birthday."

"And a lovely gift it was, too," Piper said. "Remember, I've seen pictures of you before."

Dancie gasped, and then they both laughed.

Piper finished taming Dancie's hair and while it wasn't perfect, it was an improvement. "This isn't cheating," she told Dancie as she applied some basic makeup. "Your dad will see you're making an effort to look more feminine, so subconsciously, he'll make an effort to listen. It's a sales tactic and takes nothing away from what you've accomplished."

Piper's phone buzzed. She ignored it, but Dancie reached around her and removed it from Piper's purse.

"Give me that!" Piper grabbed for the phone, but Dancie, grinning, answered it.

"Piper Scott's office. Are you ready to find your per—" Dancie abruptly stopped smiling. "I—"

Sighing, Piper said, "Put her on speaker."

Dancie pressed the screen and mouthed, "I'm sorry," as sobbing sounded from the phone.

"Piiiipeeeeerrrr!"

"I'm here." Piper kept applying makeup while a subdued Dancie held the phone.

"Dale… He's—he's gonnnnne!" More sobbing. "He left meeeeee!"

Piper squinted at Dancie's eyes and added a little more shading to one. "Did he leave you and your money or just you?"

Hiccup. "Wh-what do you mean?"

"You gave him the money, didn't you?"

"He needed it!"

"They always do." Piper didn't want to deal with this right now, which is why she hadn't answered her phone.

"But—it was for his motorcycle! He couldn't very well get to his job without his bike, could he?"

"He has a job? That's different."

Dancie winced.

"Yes, he does! In Wichita Falls."

Piper glanced at the office wall clock. Taking the phone, she handed Dancie the denim skirt and a pair of flats. Dancie was clearly feeling guilty, because she put them on without protest.

"Are you in Wichita Falls now?" Piper asked.

"No—I'm in Lubbock. Dale was going to send for me when he found us a place to live."

Piper closed her eyes and shook her head. "And he hasn't sent for you."

Sniff. "No."

"And you haven't heard from him."

"That's why I called the construction company! I thought maybe he'd been in an accident and was unconscious and—"

"They'd never heard of him." Same thing over and over again. Her mother never learned.

Sobbing.

Pointing to the clock, Dancie slipped around Piper and closed and unplugged her laptop.

"I thought he loved me!"

"You always think that," Piper said quietly. "How much, Mom?"

"Wh— That's—"

"I'm in a hurry. I've got a meeting in a few minutes. Do you have any money left at all? Or did he take you for everything?"

"Penelope Ann Scott! Don't you talk—"

Piper took her mother off speaker. "Tell me how much you need and where to send it."

When she ended the call, Dancie was trying to sneak out the door. "I'm so sorry, Piper. I never would have answered the phone—"

"Forget it." Piper planned to. Until the next time. "Put on the jacket."

"But it's *pink,*" Dancie said with heavy loathing.

"Blush khaki," Piper corrected.

"If I were the khaki, I'd blush, too."

"You wear pink." Piper indicated Dancie's tank.

"I got it at a breast-cancer awareness walkathon."

Piper slipped the jacket over her shoulders. "And now, it's complemented by the jacket." It was a lucky break that Dancie was wearing that particular tank top today.

Dancie set her computer and folder down and put on the jacket. "I'm only wearing this because I feel horrible about answering the phone."

"I know," Piper said. "But I'll take it—because you look great!" She gave Dancie a thumbs-up and followed her through the doorway.

"I didn't realize you were still sending your mom money," Dancie said as they started down the stairs.

"You have your mother issues and I have mine," Piper said. "But right now, we need to concentrate on the meeting and getting you made partner."

"Deal," Dancie said. And then, "Oh, sh—"

"Language!" Piper cautioned with a laugh.

"—oot!" Dancie finished. "Shoot, shoot, shoot!"

They were at the final turn of the staircase and Dancie was staring across the foyer at the conference table in the old dining room.

Piper followed her gaze and saw the blue-eyed limper from earlier. "Okay, who is that guy?"

"Seriously?" Dancie asked.

"Yeah, why? I ran into him earlier."

Dancie gave her a strange look. "And you didn't recognize him?"

"Well…" As they reached the bottom of the stairs, Piper glanced into the room again. "I thought he seemed vaguely familiar, but honestly? All guys are beginning to look alike to me."

"If all men look like that to you, then you're working too hard." Dancie nodded her head in his direction. "That's Mark Banning, Travis's star columnist, his big moneymaker."

There was something more… Piper couldn't quite remember.

"Oh, come on, Piper! The big-deal foreign journalist who got himself captured last year?"

"Right!" Finally, she made the connection.

"And the only reason I beat Travis in revenue is because Mark got injured. He's been teaching a journalism course at UT instead of wowing all Travis's readers with his insane adventures."

Mark got injured… Now Piper remembered. It had been all over the news. Dramatic rescue and so on. Video clips of the photogenic Mark Banning had run incessantly, including one of him waving from a stretcher, bloodstained bandage wrapped around his thigh—right about where his hand had gripped it earlier, if Piper wasn't mistaken. Ah.

Dancie exhaled. "I thought I had another quarter before I had to compete with him again." She headed for the conference room. "Well, if Mark's back, that must mean his leg has healed."

"Or maybe not," Piper murmured beneath her breath. Mark Banning had been stateside for months. If his leg was still that sensitive, then it most certainly had not fully healed.

As they walked into the room, Piper glanced at the famous Mark Banning and found him studying her in a way that meant Travis had filled him in on her identity. Not that either of them would ever have anything to do with the other—

unless Mark needed dating tips. Yeah, that wasn't going to happen. The only tip he'd need was how to fend off women, something at which he'd no doubt had a lot of practice.

He stood by the sideboard and sipped coffee, his other hand, left and ringless, for what that was worth, rested on the back of a swivel club chair. Long and lean in a leather jacket, surrounded by a cloud of confidence and testosterone. An alpha-alpha, the pinnacle of male desirability. Men wanted to be him. Women just wanted him.

Not even Piper was immune, although she had no intention of treating Mark Banning with anything other than clinical detachment.

A double-alpha male was a lot of trouble. Not only would his woman have to fight to catch him, she'd have to fight off other females to keep him. This type of man lived as though the world revolved around him because it usually did. He didn't become a part of your life, he drew you into his.

Piper would never recommend a double-alpha male for anything long-term unless a woman was a double alpha herself. And if she was, she'd hardly be a client of Piper's. The only other kind of woman for a man like that was the completely self-sacrificing type who was willing to devote her life to enhancing his—and willing to look the other way when she had to.

Believe it or not, there were women like that in the world. More power to them.

Looking at Mark Banning, Piper could understand why. He was unignorable, like a Ferrari parked among the mommobiles at a suburban grocery store—beautiful to look at and you didn't have to see it in action to know it had power and speed under the hood. Or needed extra maintenance. However, she wanted no part of a selfish, self-centered, arrogant, unaware... Except hadn't Mark opened the door for her? Twice? He hadn't said or done anything to make her feel bad when her bag had hit his leg, either. So maybe he wasn't totally self-centered and unaware, which would make him unique among the double alphas she'd interviewed. But he still had the looks and power that made her want to take him for a test drive.

"Ladies!" Travis saw them and beamed his showman smile. "May I pour you a mug of coffee?"

"You'd better, since you stole the good pot!" Dancie said to her brother.

"Just for you." Travis pushed forward an oversize mug with a crazed stick-figure woman that said, "Forget sugar and spice. Give me caffeine and then I'll be nice!"

All the other mugs were plain. It was a subtle way to diminish Dancie, who didn't notice as she eagerly gulped coffee. Piper would take care of it later.

As Travis poured more coffee, Piper looked behind the chair and saw that Mark's knee was bent and one booted toe rested on the hardwood floor. He was keeping the weight off his leg, which made her feel awful knowing her bag had bashed it.

She probably wasn't his favorite person at the moment. So why was he staring at her, clearly sizing her up?

Piper suddenly understood. She was the competition. Mark was not only the big moneymaker for Travis, he contributed to the OMG news division. At the moment, Piper was the big moneymaker for Dancie, but only wrote for the *Living Fabulous* division. However, they were presenting a proposal for expansion today and Mark was probably wondering how much of a threat to his budget she was going to be.

A lot, Piper hoped.

"Hey, Piper. How's it going?" Travis asked.

"Fine." She smiled. Travis was an alpha-beta, always striving to prove his alphaness, where a true alpha didn't need to prove anything. He wasn't her type, either.

He handed her a mug. "Good to see you, as always. You take cream and sugar?"

"Cream." It was real cream, Piper knew, because the twins' father wanted cream and not "that blue water they try to pass off as milk."

As she poured a dollop into her mug, she was aware that Mark continued to watch her. He hadn't said one word since she and Dancie had walked into the room.

Dancie must have noticed, as well. "I don't think Piper and Mark have met, Travis."

"Oh, I'm sorry." Travis touched Piper's elbow and turned her to face Mark's blue-eyed gaze. "I guess I assumed everyone knew Mark Banning."

So Travis was going to be a pain. Piper gave Mark a polite nod of recognition. "Piper Scott." She held out her hand before Travis introduced her. "We ran into each other earlier."

"And really hit it off," Mark said with an easy smile and a warm, solid grip.

She felt a flutter of attraction. Oh, he was good. "About that—"

"Don't mention it."

"Princess!" sounded from the doorway.

Mark released her hand. "Seriously," he said under his breath. "Don't mention it."

Before she could ask why, a short, older, barrel-chested man with Dancie's former nose strode into the room. B. T. Pollard, the twins' father and head of OMG. Actually, the head of several companies. He was the man who'd bankrolled the twins' college business project and expanded it into a vast online conglomerate. It had been one of his better business decisions.

"How's my baby?" He held out his arms. After planting a big kiss on Dancie's cheek, he held her hands away from her. "Look at you! Hey, Travis! Look at your sister!"

Travis gave her a thumbs-up. "Lookin' good!"

Contrary to Dancie's whining, she was wearing the perfect business-casual outfit for the occasion. The denim skirt was genius, if Piper did say so herself. And the chino khaki jacket echoed the slacks both Travis and BT wore. Honestly, even the breast-cancer awareness tank worked.

Straightened, Dancie's hair was a couple of inches longer and the ends curved just below her shoulders in a feminine wave. She could stand an eyebrow wax, but all in all, it didn't look as though she was trying to alienate her father by looking as asexual as possible.

Naturally Piper had typed B. T. Pollard for Dancie's sake—he was a beta-alpha who craved an alpha's status—and she was using all the strategies she'd learned to position him to be receptive to what Dancie had to say. Even Piper was wearing a swirly skirt, stiletto sandals, and had dug out an ancient set of hot rollers to give herself Texas big hair.

Dancie's father was as old as Piper's grandfather and clearly of the "little housewife" generation, but he loved his kids and his wife and wanted what was best for them. The problem was that he and Dancie disagreed on what was best.

Piper wished BT could see how different Dancie was from her beauty queen mother and stop trying to force her to be something she wasn't. She wished Dancie didn't care so much. Maybe if Piper had grown up with a father, she might care about gaining his approval, too.

Dancie desperately wanted to show her father that she was as valuable to the business as Travis. And Piper desperately wanted a way to pay Dancie back for all the years she'd let Piper live with her virtually rent free so Piper could stay in school. Dancie being named a partner today would do it. And then Piper could move on, guilt free.

She needed to do something different with her life, to shake things up. But what? She'd never lived anywhere but Austin and she was just…restless. Twitchy. Tired of coaching others from the sidelines. She was ready to get in the game of life, herself. That, she knew. Figuring out what she wanted was the tricky part.

Before she could stop herself, she looked at Mark Banning. He and Travis were murmuring, but while Travis watched Dancie and his father, Mark was watching her. Again. Still.

Awareness prickled her skin and she couldn't look away. Not only that, she caught herself raising her hand toward her hair. *Preening.* It was a typical female response when a woman found a man attractive. But Mark wasn't signaling romantic interest, he was studying her, no doubt looking for clues for ways he could manipulate her if he needed to. If he knew she found him attractive, then he'd use it.

Keeping that in mind, Piper stopped from touching her hair and instead grasped her mug in both hands. Then she raised the mug from waist level and held it in front of her chest. A shield—body-language talk for "I'm not interested." Which was a total lie because parts of her were shouting, "Look! Look! A prime male. Let's have *his* babies."

Mark smiled slightly and shifted his torso to face her, the rat. It signaled interest and intent and he was doing it on purpose. Piper wasn't surprised he knew something about body language. As a reporter, he'd have to.

And it was such a lovely torso, too. She wouldn't mind spending quality time with that torso, preferably without the jacket and shirt. Would it be so terrible to allow him to think he was manipulating her? Just for a little while?

No. No, no, no. Wrong game for her. Mark was a major-league all-star. Piper wasn't even ready for the minor leagues. Little League, maybe. And she'd have to warm up before she was ready to go to bat.

And Mark Banning? Who was she kidding, anyway? Talk about a guaranteed strikeout.

Why was she using sports metaphors? She didn't particularly like baseball. Maybe it was because she was standing near him and she'd breathed in some of his manly essence or something.

Oh, good grief. Dancie was seconds away from speaking to her dad in a baby voice and Piper was getting high on Mark Banning fumes.

Forcing herself to step away from him, she snagged Dancie's stupid coffee mug and walked to the sideboard where she poured coffee into a fresh mug for Dancie and another one for her. She added sugar to her own coffee because her brain needed a shot of glucose. Healthy? Not so much. Effective? Temporarily.

"Did you dress up for me?" Dancie's father leaned forward and lowered his voice. "Or have you got a boyfriend? Maybe you're meeting him for lunch?"

"Dad…" Looking embarrassed, Dancie pulled her hands away.

"Who is he? Do I know him? Maybe I'll just come along with you to lunch, eh?"

"No boyfriend," Dancie rallied. "But you can take me to lunch!" She ducked her head and a wheedling note entered her voice. "Please?" Daddy's little princess was wrapping him around her finger again.

This was not going as well as Piper had hoped.

"Aw, baby, sure, I'll take you to lunch. But what's wrong with the boys in this town? Piper—" BT addressed her for the first time "—that's your field. Tell me what's wrong with the boys in this town."

Oh, don't get me started. "Nothing, Mr. Pollard. Dancie just hasn't met the right one yet."

He gestured. "And how is she going to meet the right one when she spends all her time cooped up in front of the computer?"

Fell into that trap, didn't you, Piper?

"And her best friend is a matchmaker!" He shook his head as Dancie and Piper exchanged looks. "What kind of friend are you not to find a nice boy for my Dancie?"

"I'm not a matchmaker, Mr. Pollard. I'm a compatibility

expert. I tell women what to do after they've found a man."
Which he'd know if he ever read her column.

"Psh." He waved her away with both hands. "What's to
tell? Act like a lady and let a man be a man. Let him know
you appreciate the fact that he's a man—but not too much."

"Dad!"

He held up a thumb and finger. "A little sample," he instructed a pink-cheeked Dancie. "Leave him hungry for more
and let nature take its course."

Piper was pretty sure she heard a muffled snort from behind her. "That's a good strategy for some types of men,
though not—"

"But first she's gotta find a man! And I'm not talking about
someone like you!" BT pointed at Mark. "She needs somebody who'll be around to take care of her."

"Yes, sir." Mark spoke with complete seriousness, but beside him, Travis was about to lose it.

"Dad, I'm fine." Miraculously, Dancie had regained her
composure. "I don't need help finding a man."

BT turned back to Dancie. "You're right. They should be
finding you. Look at you. So pretty. You shouldn't be here.
You should go to lunch with your mother. Play tennis. Let
her take you around so the boys can see you."

Dancie smiled. "I'll do that."

She would?

"I'll call Mom after the meeting. Let's get started, or it'll
be too late."

Way to go, Dancie. Piper sat at the table, knowing the gen-
tlemen in the room would, too.

They did, with BT at the head, a twin on either side and
Mark and Piper facing each other across the table.

Mark had moved a little slowly, nothing anyone would have
noticed unless they were watching for it, which Piper was.
He leaned back in the cushioned chair and they locked gazes.

Let the games begin.

3

*Step three: Demonstrate kindness. The perception that
a woman is a kind person is the one trait that appeals
to all personality types.*

"OKAY." BT SLAPPED both hands on the tabletop. "Let's see
what we got here."

As he bent over to reach inside the battered leather satchel
resting on the floor next to his chair, both Dancie and Travis
emphatically mimed keeping quiet. "Don't say anything,"
Travis mouthed at Mark and included Piper with a look. She
glanced at Dancie, who had her finger to her mouth.

Okay. Got the message. Piper mimed zipping her lips.

BT tossed an old-fashioned manila folder onto the table
where it skidded a few inches across the shiny surface. The
tab was labeled in pencil Twins Biz.

Seriously? No state-of-the art electronic tablets or lap-
tops for him, which was ironic, when Piper thought about it.

BT settled his glasses in place and opened the folder. The
next few minutes passed in silence as he read and the twins
tried to decipher his expressions. An eyebrow raised here, a
head nod there, pursed lips, both eyebrows up—what a per-

formance. As if he hadn't already read and analyzed every word of the quarterly stats before the meeting.

Typical beta-alpha. Petty power games to make himself feel important. Piper amused herself by watching the others' reactions. Travis, the alpha-beta, simmered with impatience, but tried to hide it in deference to his father to whom he owed respect. Otherwise, he would have made a point of showing his contempt for those who wasted his time.

People might assume, including Piper at first, that Dancie didn't have a drop of alpha in her, but Piper suspected she might be more alpha than Travis. If Dancie wasn't so obviously desperate for validation from her father, her alpha side would be more noticeable.

And then there was Mr. Alpha-Alpha, himself.

Mark leaned back in the chair, swiveled slightly to the side, his lips curved as though amused. He probably was. Clearly, he recognized BT's posturing and was entertained by it, not annoyed. And that was the difference between Travis's type and Mark's type. Travis was irritated because he felt he had no choice but to play his father's game. If Mark no longer wanted to play the game, he simply wouldn't. He knew he could always find another boardroom in which to play and to hell—heck—with the consequences.

"So." BT sat back and removed his glasses. Tapping the folder, he said, "Travis, your sister has got some impressive numbers—even better than last quarter. Which is a good thing since your numbers are even worse than last quarter."

"Yeah." Travis gave a little chin nod toward Dancie. "Thanks for having my back while Mark's leg heals."

"I wasn't just having your back. The *Women's Guide to Living Fabulous* division is one-third of the company. Our company," Dancie emphasized. "And this year, it was the most profitable third."

Go, Dancie! She looked great, she sounded great and the stats were on her side.

Before Dancie could bring up being named a partner, Travis made his case to BT. "Back-to-college and football season always gets us a lot of hits, and then we segue right into the Super Bowl. Another popular time. By then, Mark will be back on assignment and posting his columns. If you average the phenomenal number of hits his page got during his rescue with the last few quarters, we come out ahead."

"The stats show a big drop-off in his page visitors," BT said. "What is it—eighty—ninety percent?" He threw a glance Mark's way. "How quickly they forget, eh, Mark?"

It was only as a slight color bloomed across Mark's face that Piper realized his skin had been growing paler as the meeting progressed.

He's in pain. She felt slightly sick knowing she'd contributed to it. She also noted that BT's words had made Mark angry. Really angry, judging by that gritted jaw and unblinking stare. Maybe his anger would distract him from the pain in his leg.

Before Piper could figure out what had triggered Mark's anger, Travis spoke. "His fans will come back when there's new content. And have we ever got content, right, Mark?" He gestured for Mark to speak.

Nodding, Mark rested his forearms on the table. "There's an ongoing dispute between brothers over oil rights on tribal lands in the Middle East and it appears the U.S. may be dealing with the wrong brother."

He liked to use his hands to emphasize key words when he spoke. Piper guessed it was a habit from the videos he posted online.

She heard the growing intensity in his voice as he sketched out his plans for the story. He clearly loved what he did and Piper caught herself wishing she felt the same passion about her work. It wasn't that she *disliked* what she was doing— she enjoyed helping people identify personality issues and quirks and how they affected them and those around them. Or as one of her corporate clients said, "You show us the hot buttons so we won't push them." But these days she had way more of the why-can't-I-get-a-second-date women clients than corporate consultations.

Maybe once the online Piper Plan was established, women could figure out their man problems on their own and Piper could...could... She was unable to complete the thought. And that was *her* problem.

Later. She'd puzzle it out after the meeting. For now, she'd focus on that.

Mark was finishing up his pitch. "I'm going to head over to El Bahar to investigate. If my information is true, and I think it is, then this will be huge." He sat back.

Piper believed him. How could anyone not? Negligent good looks coupled with the contained, focused intensity he'd learned speaking into webcameras equaled sincerity. People would believe anything he said. And if they were aware they were being manipulated; they wouldn't care. Piper didn't and she recognized it. Mark made people *want* to believe him. The man had charisma and an agenda, which made him dangerous.

And he was barely trying. Piper kind of wanted to see him when he was operating at full power. Maybe she'd access the OMG archives and watch a few podcasts.

"And OMG will have the exclusive," Travis was saying.

See? Mark had even distracted Piper from her objective today and she was letting them make their case for the budget dollars without a fight.

"To get the excitement started," Travis continued, "we'll be promoting the heck out of Mark's return during our Guys Annual Super Bowl Party."

Piper nudged Dancie's foot, alerting her that she shouldn't let Travis control so much of the meeting.

Dancie took the hint. "To fill the gap until Travis and Mark's numbers are up, I have a proposal to build on Piper's dating column popularity." She reached for the green folder. "There's an added advantage because it opens up a new revenue stream so my division won't be wholly dependent on ad money."

Dancie slid the green folder toward her father. "Expanding on what I said in the quarterly report, we'll have an interactive website with a software program called The Piper Plan to go along with the book—"

"Fluff," BT pronounced. "You got lucky with some female fluff." Without looking at the folder, he tossed it back at Dancie.

Fluff? BT had dismissed hundreds of hours of research as fluff? Without even looking at it? Suddenly, Mark wasn't the only one doing a slow burn. Yeah. Nothing like having your work insulted to get the juices flowing. "Mr. Pollard, my work—"

"The matchmaking business?" He raised an eyebrow. "The one that can't find my Dancie a man?"

Piper was not going to let him get to her. "It's not a dating service. I counsel clients about compatibility, particularly when management teams have to decide between equally qualified job candidates. I analyze personalities. Certain types always get along and certain types always clash. And not just romantically. My theory applies to work relationships, roommates, sports teams, careers—"

"You write a dating column for us," BT interrupted.

She wished he wouldn't keep doing that. "I— Yes." Piper exhaled. He just wouldn't let that go. "But my theory is based on extensive research."

"Your research is based on fluff."

Travis snickered, but Travis would. And Mark's reaction? Piper wasn't about to look at him because appearing to care what he thought would show weakness and she was already in a battle to be taken seriously here.

"But it's profitable fluff," Dancie said, not helping.

"Thanks a lot," Piper muttered.

"And we can make it more profitable."

"Profitable until all the air goes out of it," Travis said. "Then you've got nothing. That's why I build on the standards—your beer, your football, your barbecue—so when my fluff collapses, I've still got a safety net."

"Did you just call Mark fluff?" Piper asked. Probably unwisely. "Since you had to depend on your beer, your football and your barbecue this year."

She felt Mark's gaze laser in on her and she glanced at him. How could those blue eyes look hot and cold at the same time? She suppressed a shiver.

"Of course not." Chuckling, Travis looked at Mark, and then quickly away. "But he gives the meat, if you will, to the OMG news division and gives us…the, uh…"

"Fluff?" Piper supplied, living dangerously. She heard Dancie's breath hiss between her teeth.

A beat went by. "I give the *Guys of Texas* readers a look behind the scenes." Mark kept his gaze fastened on her. "A lot of groundwork goes into my news stories." His voice grew stronger. "News stories that change people's lives. News stories that change the world."

Implying that her work did not.

"That's a great tagline," Travis said in a fake hearty voice. "Isn't that a great tagline?" He turned to his father. "We'll have Mark at the Super Bowl with us—"

"You said he would already be overseas," Dancie added.

"Video conferencing, Dancie." Travis gave an impatient wave. "With hi-def, it's almost the same as being there in person."

"I'm glad you feel that way," BT told him. "Because you're

going to be watching the next Super Bowl on that giant big-screen TV you've got downstairs."

TRAVIS WENT STILL. "What do you mean?"

This is going to get ugly, Mark thought. Travis did love his Super Bowl parties.

BT leaned forward. "I mean that the salary for Mark's new partner is coming out of your Super Bowl budget."

Partner? Mark didn't like where this was going.

"What new partner?" Travis turned to Mark. "You didn't say anything about—"

"Thanks," Mark said to BT. "But I don't need a partner. I'll be fine."

"Good to hear. But you're still going to be working with a partner."

Never. "I work alone."

BT shook his head. "Not anymore. You take too many risks, Mark."

So he'd heard. "That's how I get stories nobody else does. They hesitate. Hang back. Or they have to wait for authorization. I go for it."

"Sometimes you shouldn't."

"Sometimes I don't. You never hear about those times."

"I sure did last year." BT drew a long breath.

Here it comes. The man was entitled to a lecture, Mark supposed. BT hadn't said a whole lot at the time Mark had been rescued. Then again, he'd been injured and, as Travis had pointed out, getting a lot of media attention. But that was last year and BT clearly wanted to assert his authority before sending Mark back into the field.

So be it. Mark would take the verbal spanking, apologize, and then they could get back to business, although he'd prefer not to have this conversation in front of Travis's sister's and Piper's assessing gaze.

Mark sensed that she wasn't impressed by him. That bothered him some and being bothered annoyed him. Usually, Mark didn't care what strangers thought of him. *Maybe it's because you hope she won't stay a stranger.*

Where did that come from? She wasn't his usual type and Mark would bet he wasn't hers, either. He couldn't imagine a reason for them to see each other again after today. He wasn't going to seek her out. What would be the point, when he'd be half a world away in a couple of months?

"On your last assignment, you ignored State Department warnings," BT said, starting his lecture, and Mark refocused his attention. "You ignored my direct order to break off contact with Mendoza."

Because I do not take orders from someone who has no idea of the situation. Not too fond of orders, period. "You weren't there. If you'd seen what I—"

"It doesn't matter what you saw," BT interrupted. "You were taken hostage and as far as the government was concerned, you'd ignored their warning, so it was tough luck."

This was old ground and they didn't need to cover it again. "Meeting with Mendoza was a risk I was willing to take," Mark said.

BT jabbed a finger to his chest. "But I wasn't!"

"Dad," Travis interrupted. "He gets it. Let's move on."

BT silenced his son with a look. "Mark, your decision cost me hours of my life dealing with petty bureaucrats and not so petty bureaucrats. You're only here now because Travis raised money from the *Guys of Texas* readers to hire mercenaries to go into those mountains and get you."

Yeah, and the No Guy Left Behind project got a huge amount of news coverage in the process. It was a brilliant strategy that resulted in soaring ad revenue. Not only that, it had succeeded, for which Mark was grateful. "And I appreciate that."

"We're good, Dad," Travis said.

"But I'm not good," BT retorted. "I'm not good at all.

Mark's reckless—the kind of reckless I can't afford." Pointing at Mark, he continued, "If you had a wife or a girlfriend, we wouldn't be having this conversation. They wouldn't let you get away with the crazy risks you take." He gave a short laugh and nodded toward Piper. "Maybe you should talk to this one about finding you a girlfriend."

Mark flicked a glance her way.

"Not a matchmaker," Piper said.

"Whatever you call yourself." BT was insultingly dismissive.

Mark could understand why the man was angry at him, but from what Travis had told him, Piper Scott had been responsible for a nice uptick in OMG's bottom line.

"Mark, the point is, if you had a partner to answer to, you'd think twice."

That didn't sound like a partner; that sounded like a babysitter. "Thinking twice is how reporters miss stories." He shifted, deliberately softening his body language. "I chose to work at OMG because you gave me a freedom other journalists envy. In return, my reporting has enhanced OMG's reputation—and profits."

Mark hated playing the money card, but it always came down to money.

"And he's ready to do it again, too." Travis slapped the arms of his chair, mimicking one of his father's gestures. "I say we stick with what works for him."

"But it's not working for me." BT leaned forward and laced his fingers together, telegraphing that he wasn't budging.

Hell. It had been a good run at OMG. He hated to see it end.

Out of the corner of his eye, Mark saw a movement and knew Travis's sister and Piper had exchanged a look. They knew what was coming, too.

"Mark." BT gazed steadily at him. "This hasn't been the first time you've stepped on governmental toes. I've got a budget item called 'news support services' that's nothing but money I use for bribes—excuse me—fines to either get you out of a mess or ensure the local authorities leave you alone. You disappear for days at a time without checking in. You change your travel plans without telling anyone. I think you're in one country and you pop up in another. You ignore me and, frankly, without somebody riding herd on you, you're not worth the liability, aggravation and expense."

"Dad!" Travis looked genuinely shocked.

Mark had been worth it before and he'd be worth it again. This was all about Travis's father showing everybody who was boss. Mark didn't mind up to a point, but forcing a partner on him was that point. "I work alone."

"I'll take the responsibility, Dad," Travis offered.

Sounded like a plan to Mark. He nodded his thanks to Travis.

BT shook his head. "You're not part of the news division. You'd have to get up to speed on everything we're doing and you're overloaded now."

"It seems as though Mark isn't the only one who needs a partner," Dancie said.

"I *work* alone." Mark subtly shifted the emphasis.

"Make me an OMG partner and I can take some of the extra responsibilities from Travis," Dancie offered. "I could handle Mark."

That was the most alarming thing Mark had heard so far.

Travis slowly shook his head. "Oh, nooooo, you couldn't."

"There's not going to be any extra work because I'm sending someone with him. Okay, Mark, let's call it a producer, since you don't work with a partner," BT said. "A female, because I don't want two men getting into a pissing contest. Pardon my French, ladies. But it's gotta be a woman who can stand up to him."

A woman? It kept getting worse. "I work *alone*." This time the emphasis wasn't subtle.

No one paid any attention to Mark. He wasn't accustomed to being ignored—at least not as an adult.

But the twins were now arguing with their father. Travis was going to bat for him, and he appreciated it, but no way was he going to be handicapped by a handler. A woman? He lived pretty rough when he was in the field. And taking a woman to the Middle East would be just insane.

BT was right about one thing, though. The reason Mark wasn't involved in a relationship was precisely because he put himself in situations no family man should.

The Pollards grew louder as the discussion became more heated. Unless BT could be talked out of his producer edict, this was a massive waste of Mark's time and he had a one o'clock class he needed to prep for.

He looked across the table. Piper also sat silently while the Pollards hashed things out. She was mad, though, and rightly so.

Her profile was to him, so Mark took the opportunity to check her out. She wore square glasses with dark frames the way pretty women sometimes did when they wanted to be taken seriously. And she was pretty, in a church picnic kind of way, the sort of girl his grandmother would like. Sweetly pastel and prim. Too girlie for his mom, though. And to be honest, for him, as well. A life with her would mean drinking tea from china cups and taking off his shoes before he walked on the carpet. At least that's the impression he got. Mark had no personal experience with her type. He smiled to himself. Her type avoided his type.

She must have sensed him looking at her, because she slowly turned her head and met his stare with one of her own.

Big brown eyes gazed directly at him from behind the glasses. That was no Sunday-school stare. And now that he thought about it, there hadn't been any coyness about her the other times they'd studied each other. Mark felt a stirring of interest. There was something more here. Hidden depths. And nobody loved hidden depths more than Mark.

"Coffee?" she mouthed slowly. Her upper teeth dragged over her bottom lip drawing his attention to its plump pinkness.

Something else stirred as his interest shifted from intellectual to physical. Had she done that on purpose? If so, then she was Sunday school on the outside and Saturday-night party on the inside. Every man's fantasy woman.

He nodded in answer to her coffee question and nudged his mug across the table. Rather than take it to the credenza, Piper reached behind her for the thermal pot. Doing so stretched her top across her chest. Nice.

Yeah, *nice*. Remember that. Nice girl. Okay, nice girl with some moves.

Piper leaned forward to pour the coffee and the V-neck of her top gaped enough for Mark to take in nicely rounded flesh and some lace. The coffee filled his mug in a slow stream that gave him plenty of time to stare down her top and plenty of time for her to be aware of it.

He might be in a little trouble here. He hadn't been with a woman in way too long. Between his injury and the off-limits students, he'd had to freeze those urges. Piper Scott was definitely thawing them and at a most inconvenient time.

He forced his eyes downward a few more inches so they were focused on the coffee mug and not on Piper Scott's surprisingly deep, lace-outlined cleavage.

The instant he saw the spout of the coffeepot tilt back, Mark grasped his mug and risked a glance upward, aiming for Piper's eyes without traveling over her breasts. "Thanks."

She smiled in response, and he smiled back because it would be impolite not to.

But then her smile grew and he knew she'd caught him looking down her top. She'd flashed him deliberately as repayment for their little thing earlier, before the meeting started, when they'd been sizing each other up.

Nicely played. Grinning, he dipped his head and raised his mug a fraction of an inch in acknowledgement. And then their gazes connected in one of those "hey, there could be something here" moments. Finding out could be fun. But Mark's style was intense and temporary, no muss, and no fuss when his work ended the relationship.

Too bad Piper Scott wasn't the type. Too bad one of the more attractive things about her was that she knew it.

The connection lasted long enough for both of them to realize nothing was going to happen between them and feel a twinge of regret—well, Mark sure did.

BT interrupted the moment by roaring, "Enough!"

Piper flinched and set the coffeepot down.

"You—" BT pointed at Mark. "I don't care what you call her, but you're taking somebody on assignment with you from now on. And you will consult with that somebody and if you don't, I'll pull your press credentials. And you—" he pointed to Piper. "If you and Dancie want OMG's backing for your project, then show me this compatibility theory of yours works. Find Mark somebody he can get along with and who can stand up to him. That last part is very important."

"Dad, get serious!" Travis nearly came out of his chair. "She's a dating columnist! We're talking about hiring somebody who's going to be working with a world-class journalist, not finding Mark a date to the prom!" He didn't bother to hide his scorn, which Mark could have told him was a mistake.

Sure enough, the women were eyeing Travis with narrow-eyed gazes. "The way it works is that you only send me qualified candidates," Piper said in clipped tones. "I'll select the most compatible ones from among those."

Not going to happen. Mark shook his head, but Piper didn't notice. Or if she did, she ignored him.

"And when am I supposed to find the time to do that?"

Travis asked. "Since we're not going to the Super Bowl—" he sent a resentful glance toward his father "—I have to redo *everything*. And that includes contacting the advertisers—"

"I can help you out, Travis," Dancie offered sweetly.

Mark had heard enough. "Don't bother," he said. "For the last time, I. Work. Alone."

"Not if you're working at OMG," BT told him.

Which is pretty much how Mark had expected this to play out. BT should be the one interviewing employees for the news division. He hadn't said anything about doing so because he knew it wasn't going to happen.

"Fair enough." Mark pushed back from the table. "I'll always be grateful for the opportunities OMG gave me."

"Hang on a minute, Mark." Panic sounded in Travis's voice.

Mark stood, his leg screaming in protest. "Travis, it's time for me to move on." Past time for a pain pill, too. "Bye, all."

Travis swiveled his chair away from the table. "Mark, wait."

Mark pushed open the door. "I'll call you later." He had to get off his leg. Limping badly, he started across the foyer, knowing there was a real possibility he might not make it to his car.

"I've got a client meeting," he heard behind him. "So I'm going to leave now, too."

In an instant, Piper was beside him. "Lean on me," she murmured beneath her breath. She held out her arm in a way that hid it from those in the conference room behind them.

He wasn't about to argue. Bracing himself against her took some of the weight off his leg and relieved the pain.

"It stiffened up in the meeting, didn't it?" she asked.

"Yeah," he grunted. "Thanks."

"Can you walk to the front door?"

Mark gave a tight nod.

"Whenever you're ready."

He started walking and she matched her steps to his, bless her, and as soon as they were out of sight, she insisted he lean on her fully.

Mark was relieved that she didn't try to make conversation. If it hadn't been for his damned leg, he would have appreciated her closeness more.

As they negotiated a couple of steps, he inhaled sharply and smelled her perfume. It was a flowery, sweet, girlie scent he wouldn't have associated with her, especially in a business situation. But now that she was pressed up against him, he noticed the jewelry and the hair and the skirt and especially the sandals with the high heels. She looked as though she was going out on a date. Or entering a beauty pageant.

Or dressing to appeal to BT, clever girl.

So she wasn't necessarily the church picnic type.

"Where are you parked?" she asked as he wondered about her normal style.

"Faculty lot near the Burns building."

"Where's your class?"

"Burns building."

"And where are your pain meds?"

He stopped and looked down at her, but instead was visualizing the orange plastic container in his gym bag.

Piper met his gaze. "I'm guessing you either didn't fill the prescription because you don't like the idea, or you left them at home or some other inconvenient place."

She had him pegged. "They're in my locker at the physical therapy center." Which was several miles away. He could have used the campus facilities for his rehab, but didn't want an audience when he worked out.

"Okay, then we will get you to the Burns building for your class and you will give me the key to your locker and I will get the meds." She wasn't asking; she was telling, step by no-nonsense step.

Mark didn't like being told what to do and how to do it even if he agreed. "You should go back to the meeting."

She glanced behind her. "It's all over but the shouting. Literally. Now give me your key and I'll drive to the PT center and get your pain medication."

Need and pride warred within him.

Her expression never changed and she spoke in the same nursery-school teacher tone. "You wouldn't need them if it wasn't for me. If you don't give me the chance to make it right, I'll feel awful."

"You are so lying." He shook his head, grinning down at her. "You didn't even try to sell that."

"I have no idea what you're talking about." She batted her eyes.

"Your blatant attempt to let me save face. Thanks, anyway." He looked at her a moment longer, and then grimaced. "I hurt. Help me to the Burns building, and then I'm taking you up on your offer to get my pills. When you get back, I don't care if class has started or not. Walk right on up and hand them to me. I'll make sure I have a bottle of water."

4

Step four: Time the end of your first encounter to leave him intrigued.

WITH AUSTIN TRAFFIC being what it was and men's locker rooms being what they were, Piper's drive to the PT center to retrieve Mark's pain pills took longer than she'd hoped.

But because it took longer, she had a chance to think about this morning. And to think about him.

Piper hadn't quite figured Mark out. Talk about refreshing. She still identified him as a double alpha, with exceptions. When a man racked up several exceptions, it was time to consider placing him in a different category. But Mark didn't fit in any other category. He might be a whole new category. Wouldn't that be a kick?

Then again, he could be faking it. While people could mask their true personality, Piper usually sensed when they were doing so. Also, they only masked when they had to or when they were being observed. Mark was effortlessly alpha. And yet…

He'd called her on lying to him. She had been. And he knew why—and he'd thanked her. That was cool of him. And unexpected. He'd accepted her help without protesting and admitted that he hurt.

An alpha revealing vulnerability? Pain was obviously a factor, but he seemed more aware of other people than his type usually was.

Take the meeting. Yeah, two hours of her life she'd never get back. But during the excruciating time when BT was scolding him, he just took it. Someone else might have thought Mark was chastened, but Piper knew he didn't consider it worth the effort to push back. BT needed to vent and Mark's ego was fine with letting him do so.

She could find him a compatible partner, if he wanted her to. Filling a vacancy in an established team or group was something she'd done before. Mark was a team of one, but the principles were the same. It was too bad he wouldn't consider the proposition. She would have liked to prove her theories.

Oh, admit it. You just want an opportunity to spend more time with him. And it is not just because you have something to prove. Although there was that.

BT dismissing her work as fluff wasn't surprising, but dismissing it without reading Dancie's proposal? That was a mistake made by a man who didn't make those kinds of mistakes. Delivering an ultimatum to Mark was another. Men like Mark never responded to ultimatums the way those making them wanted or expected. Any time it was "my way or the highway," they'd take the highway every time.

As Piper circled the Burns building in hopes of finding a parking spot—very unlikely without a faculty tag—she remembered teasing Mark with the coffeepot. Totally inappropriate. But fun. When was the last time she'd had that kind of fun? When was the last time she'd been out with a man on a purely social basis? Or wanted to be? Lately, Piper found men boringly predictable. Within a minute, she could place them into one of her infamous grid squares and know exactly what they were going to say and do.

But not Mark.

Her stomach did a little flip. Ooh, this wasn't good. He could really get to her if she let him. Not that she'd let him. Or that he'd try.

There had been a moment, several seconds when they'd smiled at each other and Piper, lost in the unexpectedness of it all, considered some what-ifs. Like, what if he wasn't returning to his vagabond ways? And what if she ignored the fact that he was precisely the wrong type for her? And what if she wasn't misinterpreting those few seconds and he actually was interested in her? And what if she might not be making the same mistake she'd seen her mother make over and over by getting involved with him?

Yeah. Those what-ifs.

Piper circled the building twice before giving up and driving toward the parking garage several blocks away.

Getting involved with Mark—even assuming it was an option—would not end well. And it would end. She even knew when. So the best strategy for her right now was to park her car, walk several blocks to the building and interrupt his class, which would definitely have started by the time she got there. Then she'd go see Dancie and pick up the pieces. Although, now that she thought about it, she wasn't sure there would be any pieces to pick up. Dancie seemed to be handling her father's refusal awfully well.

Piper found a spot on the next-to-the-top level of the garage, but at least she found a spot. The Burns building was a fifteen-minute jog away. Changing into a pair of flat sandals she kept in the car for situations like this, she took the elevator to the street level and looked for a campus shuttle stop.

Although she caught a shuttle, she didn't gain a whole lot of time. It was 1:20 when she walked through the door of the Burns building. Mark would be well into his class.

Ethics in Foreign Journalism was held in the largest lecture hall and when Piper peeked in the back, she saw it was a full house. Easily two hundred and fifty to three hundred students sat in the tiers. And down below, sitting on a stool on the stage in front of a projection screen, was Mark. He'd ditched the leather jacket and wore a pale blue, button-down shirt with the cuffs rolled back. There was a small table next to him. Even all the way from the back, Piper could see the bottle of water.

Seriously? He wanted her to waltz across a *stage* and give him drugs in front of his students? No way. She'd find a side entrance, get his attention and signal him to come to her.

That's right, she thought as she made her way around the building, *make a man with a bum leg limp off the stage because you feel weird about walking out there in front of all those people and giving him his pills.* Obviously, she wasn't going to do that. And after she gave him his pills, then what? Was he just going to stop, pop some pain meds in front of his class and go on lecturing? He'd have to tell them what the medication was for. Had he considered that?

Piper found the side entrance, helpfully labeled Lecture Platform, and cracked the door. It opened directly into the room. No hall or foyer. No way to sneak in. She stepped inside and several heads turned her way, including Mark's. Without stopping his lecture, he beckoned to her.

Piper climbed the steps to the platform. As she made her way toward him, Mark twisted off the cap of the water bottle. "Here's a bonus tip—getting shot hurts. Getting stabbed hurts."

Piper handed him the pill bottle.

"Trust me, the ratings are not worth it." As the students laughed lightly, he shook out a pill and swallowed it. "Thanks," he said and gave her a quick smile.

Up close, he didn't look so hot. Oh, sure, he had journalist-chic nailed, but the strain showed on his face and the dark hollows of his eyes.

"The label says to take two," Piper suggested when he started to set the pill container on the table.

He glanced at her and touched his lapel mike to turn it off. "One or two as needed."

"You need it."

His expression grew impatient. "I'll take another if I have to."

Piper stayed put even though the room had gone quiet. "I'm sure you've been told that you've got to stay ahead of the pain. Right now, I'll bet it's way ahead of you."

They stared at each other. Hollowed eyes or not, Mark's stare packed a wallop.

What was it to her whether he hurt or not? His leg had been bothering him before their run-in this morning and it would continue to bother him. He wasn't her responsibility and it was presumptuous to challenge him in front of his students. And yet here she was, staring him down.

"You're going to stand here until I take another pill, aren't you?" he asked.

"Yes." Looking at his face, Piper felt an overwhelming urge to mother him. Not the emotion she'd expect to have for a man who embodied the male ideal and was breathtakingly handsome besides. But definitely safer.

Piper heard a few whispers among the class.

"It wouldn't bother me if you did stay here," Mark told her.

"Yes, it would." Piper gave him a slow smile. "I'd make sure of it."

Surprise registered in the depths of those blue eyes. They went a little smoky as his gaze flicked over her face and lingered on her mouth. "Tempting."

And didn't that one word define the two of them so far? It would be tempting to find out if the pleasure now would be worth the pain later and she wasn't talking about here on the lecture platform.

Now, *that* was her more immediate concern, because

she'd just recklessly issued an ultimatum to a man who didn't respond to ultimatums.

Turning his lapel mike back on, he spoke to the restless students. "We'll be discussing the photograph on page one-hundred-seven of the big print book I made you lug to class today. If one of you will kill the lights, I'll put the first version up on the screen." He pressed the remote and a photograph appeared behind him.

Oops. She was going to look pretty dumb standing here for the next half hour. Or she could wimp out and slink away.

But during the rustling as students flipped through their oversize text book, Mark gazed straight at her and took the second pill.

Or maybe he'd palmed it. She wasn't going to ask. She was off the hook. He'd done it her way so she could hit the highway. Piper gave him a thumbs-up, smiled a goodbye and turned to leave.

"Hey."

She felt his fingers on her bare forearm. Awareness radiated from the point of contact.

He blinked as though he felt it, too, and brought his hand to his mike. "I appreciate this." A beat went by. "I guess I'll see you around."

For a moment there, she'd sensed he'd been going to say something more.

But he hadn't.

Piper nodded and by the time she climbed off the platform, Mark was already lecturing again.

So that was that. It was for the best. Really. Absolutely. She'd take the win and get out.

Except, when Piper reached the exit door, she couldn't make herself go through it. Sometimes the best option was boring and wasn't she tired of being bored?

Hidden by the dim light, she made her way along the side aisle to the back of the hall. There wasn't a single empty seat that she could see, so she stood by the double doors in the back.

What am I doing? She needed to call Dancie and she'd missed lunch, but here she was, standing in the back of a lecture hall to listen to a man she'd never see again. At least not in person. Unless...

Oh, this was an inconvenient attraction. He was a triple threat. He attracted her physically, was turning out to be surprisingly likeable, and intrigued her professionally. Throw in those few moments of connection and there was a very good chance that if Piper didn't walk away and forget about him, she'd end up doing something stupid.

She'd walk away later. The forgetting part might take a few days.

Mark was showing how the photograph of a man giving a speech had appeared in three different publications. Each publication had cropped it in a way that illustrated opposing points of view.

"If this version was all you saw, you'd think the speaker had a huge audience." Mark advanced to the next frame and the students murmured.

Piper saw that what had been cropped out was the ticket booth where the people were waiting in line to get into a street festival. They weren't part of the speaker's audience at all.

The next frame showed the picture cropped heavily to the left, showing the speaker surrounded by the press. The frame after that revealed that behind the press was open space, not an audience. In fact, it appeared that the whole thing was a staged speech for an advertisement and not a news event at all.

The next frame showed the speaker surrounded by an applauding, sign-carrying audience who clearly liked what they were hearing.

"You can see how an editor's agenda can alter perception." Mark changed the screen. "And this is the actual photograph in its entirety."

There were sounds of surprise as the photograph revealed a man off to the side holding a large placard that said Applaud If You Want a Free Soft Drink!

"But wait, there's more," he said teasingly. "Here's video of the scene before and after that photograph was taken. It was shot by me from my hotel room balcony."

With the rest of the class, Piper watched as the speaker arrived and a crowd of a few dozen at most was packed together and directed when to applaud and fed questions to ask. Then, they were moved to a different side and handed signs so photographers could shoot from another angle. The video fast-forwarded through more stagings and then returned to normal speed to show campaign workers handing white cards to those in the crowd.

"Watch what happens," Mark instructed.

The people got in line for their free soft drinks, and then exchanged their cards for entry to the street festival.

"They were paid!" someone said.

"Yes." Mark paused. "Because they were participating in the filming of a campaign video."

There was a buzz of comments before someone asked, "So what's wrong with that?"

"Not a thing," Mark said. "Unless a lazy reporter for a wire service uses the photo to illustrate an actual campaign stop. Which is what happened here. That picture was propagated as fact through the news media. Even worse, the photo was cropped to be flattering or unflattering, according to the views of various editors. Finally, somebody who bothered to dig noticed that the photo existed prior to the event it was supposed to illustrate. And that was the beginning of what became one of the ugliest media scandals of the last decade."

A student raised her hand. "What happened to the reporter who used the picture?"

"Eventually, everyone at that bureau was fired or resigned," Mark answered.

"What about the reporter who uncovered the story?" another asked.

"He became a foreign correspondent."

He's talking about himself. Piper wondered if the students would figure it out.

There were other questions but Piper quit listening and just watched Mark. It was hard not to. He sat with a casual ease, one foot on the rung of the stool. No one would ever guess he was in pain. It was an impressive display of self-control.

She wondered what drove him and what it would take for him to commit to a woman. One woman. Not a hook up, but a life mate.

She wasn't that woman. *Tempting,* he'd said. Oh, yeah. She'd like to spend quality time with Mark Banning although he was completely wrong for her. She wanted stability and commitment and he wanted to bounce around the world by himself. Where was a relationship between them likely to lead? To her waving goodbye as his plane took off, that's where. Why was she tempted by something she knew would hurt her? Did she think she could change him?

Maybe she was more like her mother than she thought. Except her mother always gave in to temptation and Piper would not.

Men did not change.

She stressed this over and over and over again to her dating clients. Fall in love with the man as he is, not who you want him to be.

She checked her phone for the time. The class was almost over, which meant Dancie would probably be back from lunch with her mother. Piper had blocked out today to work with Dancie in anticipation of getting the go-ahead to launch the Piper Plan website, but that was toast. Dancie was probably a basket case. Clearly, the situation called for a bittersweet chocolate croissant with mocha cream spread or a pitcher of margaritas. Too bad it was too early for the margaritas. An argument might be made that it was never too early for margaritas, but Piper wasn't going to make it. With a last glance at Mark, and a little sigh for what might have been, Piper slipped out the back of the lecture hall and headed for the Croissant Cafe.

MARK WAS AWARE OF the exact moment Piper left, just as he'd been aware of her presence during his lecture. Had she stayed because she'd been interested or because she wanted to make sure he wasn't going to keel over?

Feeling regret that he'd never know, Mark finished answering the students' questions, dismissed the class and stayed for the obligatory ten minutes when he was surrounded by starry-eyed young women.

It was always the female students who lingered, and Mark had learned that if he didn't hang out with them until the professor for the next class arrived, they'd line up outside his office.

He owed Piper Scott big-time. He would have been in major trouble without the meds. He was even willing to admit that she'd been right about taking two pills. As the pain became manageable, he felt other muscles he'd been tensing relax. He didn't experience the spaciness or brain fog he'd dreaded, either. In fact, he'd been able to think more clearly without actively fighting the pain.

Yeah, he probably should have taken a dose prior to this morning's meeting. Maybe it would have even turned out differently. Maybe he could have convinced BT to give him a second chance instead of concentrating on hiding the fact that he hadn't healed as quickly as he'd pretended.

But he hadn't; so now Mark was moving on.

Thankfully, the other professor arrived a few minutes early. Mark nodded a goodbye to the girls, grabbed his laptop and water bottle, and walked gingerly, but without help, to his office.

With relief, he closed the door and drew a deep breath. He could still smell Piper's perfume. Her curves had fit against him in all the right places and she'd been exactly the right height when he'd gripped her shoulder to take the weight off his leg. As they'd walked, he'd shifted more of his weight. She hadn't flinched and never mentioned it.

He liked her. Maybe too much. Not many people would have stared him down in front of his students until he'd taken the second pill. He'd been tempted to call her bluff and make her stand next to him for the rest of the class, but he figured she was the type to make good on her threat to bother him.

She already bothered him. Crossing to the desk, he lowered himself onto the chair and inhaled once more. He needed to stop thinking about Piper Scott and get on with finding another job. If this had been another time and another place…

But it wasn't.

So Mark opened his laptop and phone and started calling his contacts. The sooner he got affiliated with a news bureau, the sooner the clock on his non-compete clause would start ticking. Maybe if he kept writing columns for Travis, BT would waive the clause.

Seven calls later, Mark plugged his phone into the charger and sat back in the chair to regroup.

He'd hit all the big names and nobody had anything for him. Nothing. What had happened to all the "if you're ever available, give us a call" offers? He was available. He was calling.

Maybe instead of selling himself, he should sell the story. But why should he have to? He was Mark Banning, damn it. BT's words echoed in his mind. *How quickly they forget, eh, Mark?*

An uncomfortable feeling settled in his stomach. Nobody was going to forget him. Mark would pay his own expenses to travel to the Middle East, if he had to. But he needed press credentials. Good ones, not freelancer ones bought off the internet.

So maybe he'd have to accept a position with a lower-tier news agency. He didn't care. With Mark Banning on the roster, an agency wouldn't remain lower tier for long.

Mark studied his list of contacts, eliminating anyone who hadn't tried to poach him from OMG.

"Wally Shetland, I'm about to make your day." He'd met Wally a couple of times at press junkets. Wally had never been affiliated with one of the majors, so he usually ended up in the back of the room. With Mark on board, Wally would have access to the front row.

He brought up the regional news service's website on his laptop, studied it for a few minutes and, using the landline, punched in the phone number.

Wally, himself, answered the phone. The outfit must be smaller than Mark thought.

"Hey, Mark," Wally said after Mark identified himself. "University of Texas comes up on caller ID. What's the problem? Afraid I wouldn't take your call?"

Weird comment. "I'm teaching a course here this semester," Mark explained. "Why wouldn't you want to take my call?"

"You've been calling a lot of people this afternoon. I gotta tell you, I'm hurt I wasn't farther up on your list."

Word had spread that Mark was job hunting. Bunch of gossips. Wally should be glad he was on Mark's list at all. "So you already know OMG and I have parted ways."

"Oh, yeah."

That wasn't encouraging.

Mark wondered what story was going around, but he wasn't going to ask. "I've got a lead on a great piece."

"You always do," Wally said. It didn't sound like a compliment.

Mark continued, "I'm offering *Phoenix Regional* an exclusive."

Wally snorted. "Nobody else was interested. Why should I be?"

This wasn't the reaction Mark had expected, but he could understand why Wally would be suspicious of Mark Banning offering an exclusive to a small-time media outlet. "I haven't offered anyone else this story." Mark heard the muffled clicking of a computer keyboard. The guy wasn't emailing while they were talking, was he? "You're the first and only, Wally."

"Yeah, right."

"True fact." A little humor there. "I like the latitude smaller outfits give me. And this story will take time to develop."

Unbelievably, Wally hesitated. See, that was the problem too many people had. A Mark Banning exclusive would bump Wally up to the next level. Top tier. But this hesitation was why he hadn't progressed further in their mutual field than he had.

"You'd be attached to it, I assume." Wally hadn't asked anything about the story.

"You say that like it's a bad thing." The uneasy feeling Mark had dismissed as his stomach's reaction to the medication strengthened. This was his gut telling him something was wrong.

Another hesitation. "I'm going to level with you, Mark, because nobody else has the cojones. So here it is—nobody is going to touch you. You've got a reputation as a loose cannon. With all the shaky stuff going on politically, and the liability issues, and shrinking budgets, the networks and bureaus can't take a chance that you'll go rogue and end up costing them."

Fear was dictating news stories now? What had happened to his profession? "You'd think no reporter had ever been taken hostage before. Just FYI, it's not an experience I intend to repeat."

He heard Wally exhale and then background noises became muffled before there was the sound of a door closing. "Mark, buddy."

Mark squashed the thought that he and Wally had never been buddies.

"I want to help you out. I *really* do, but I'd lose my job."

Lose his job? For hiring Mark? The guy was telling the truth; Mark could hear it in his voice. He was persona non grata. Blacklisted. And everyone had known it except Mark.

The realization felt just like when his captors had kicked him.

BT had known it, too, which put him in a position to set the conditions for Mark's next assignment. No wonder he'd let Mark walk. He'd enjoy making Mark grovel before taking him back, too.

If he took him back.

When Mark said nothing, Wally went on. "I'm going to give you a piece of advice. And I'm speaking as someone who has admired your career. Stay out of the spotlight for a while. Keep your gig at UT. Or write a book. Do both, even. Then ease back into it, maybe do a couple of documentaries."

"Documentaries?" Mark couldn't believe he was hearing this.

"They're not that bad."

Mark closed his eyes.

"You need to prove you're not wild-man Banning anymore. Give it a few years and try getting back into the field then."

"When everyone has forgotten me?" His chest grew tight.

Wally laughed. "You'll remind them."

"Well, thanks for the advice," Mark forced himself to say.

"Hey—send me an autographed copy of the book when it comes out, okay?"

"Absolutely." Mark barely avoided slamming the phone back into the cradle. Hang ups on a landline could be so much more dramatic than when using a cell phone.

Mark stared at the computer screen for several long minutes before closing the file with the list of contacts. He'd only humiliate himself by calling anyone else.

He owed Wally. He hadn't liked what the guy had said, but appreciated the guts it took to say it. Mark also knew it was absolutely the truth. He was untouchable. More than anything Wally said, it was what he hadn't that convinced Mark. Not once during their entire conversation had Wally asked about the story. That was because no story was worth hiring Mark Banning.

How had this happened? He'd messed up *one* time...okay, more than once, but getting captured was by far the worst. Or had he just been unaware of the reputation he was earning?

Not entirely, but he hadn't cared because OMG hadn't cared, either. Until now.

If he wanted an assignment, it looked as though he was going to have to put up with a handler. Always assuming OMG would take him back and that was by no means a sure thing.

Fine. He'd go find a "producer," but it would be on his terms. Mark opened and closed drawers, looking for a piece of paper and a marker. He ended up ripping a page out of a student exam booklet and writing *Job Opportunity* in block letters across the top. He thought for a minute and ripped out another piece of paper to write *Journalism Internship.* That would make it clear who was in charge.

"'Mark Banning has agreed,'" he spoke as he wrote, "'to take an intern with him on his next assignment. If you're interested, leave your résumé along with 250 words explaining why he should select you for this *once-in-a-lifetime opportunity*—'" he underlined that part "'—in the box outside room 10B.'"

Now all he had to do was make some copies and find a box.

5

Step five: Arrange a "chance" encounter with your per-fect man. It should be brief and unexpected—at least for him.

PIPER STOPPED OUTSIDE Dancie's office and listened. No weep-ing and wailing and stomping around the room. In fact, Piper walked in to find Dancie industriously typing on her com-puter.

She looked absolutely fine, therefore something must be terribly wrong. Piper braced herself. "Hey, how was lunch with your mom?"

Dancie kept typing. "It was great."

Great? Lunch with her mother had been great? Truly great and not sarcastic great?

It seemed so. Piper was not certain how to proceed, since the meeting with BT followed by lunch with her mother should have meant Dancie was having a Very Bad, Horri-ble, Awful Day.

Maybe she was in shock.

Piper dragged a chair next to Dancie's desk and set the box of croissants within reach.

Dancie hit Save and looked up. "Ooh. I'll pass. I'm still

full from lunch. Hey, did you know there's this hair thing they can do that'll keep your hair straight for weeks? It takes hours and is superexpensive, but your hair will look really great. I've got an appointment next Wednesday."

Piper stared at her longtime friend. Then she opened the box of croissants, took one and stuffed half of it into her mouth.

"Piper! What are you doing?"

Piper pointed to her mouth.

"Well, yeah, I see that. I meant why?"

Piper swallowed. "I missed lunch?"

"What have you been doing?" Dancie's eyes widened and she answered her own question. "You've been with Mark Banning all this time?"

Piper nodded. Shouldn't they be talking about Dancie? Piper was supposed to be sympathizing and propping up Dancie's self-confidence. That was the way it always worked.

"Spill it," Dancie demanded.

Well, okay. Piper told her, even about the mutual connection thing.

Dancie didn't like the mutual connection thing. She started shaking her head before Piper finished. "Don't fall for him."

"I don't intend to." Piper gazed at the other half of the croissant in her hand. *Tempting.* Bumping into Mark, Mark at the meeting, helping a Mark in pain, staring him down in front of his class—and winning, hearing him lecture…she'd packed a whole lot of Mark into a few hours.

"But he intrigues me," she admitted before eating the other half of the croissant.

"You're kidding." Dancie's eyes grew round and her mouth dropped open. "You're not kidding! Oh, come on!"

"What?"

"He is completely wrong for you and you know it."

She did. "I said *intrigued,* not infatuated."

"He's getting to you," Dancie insisted. "I can't believe it.

You know every male move in the book. Hell—heck… Oh, wait. I can say *hell* now. Hell, you *wrote* the book!"

Piper almost choked over a laugh before she could swallow. "Well, you know, there is the chemistry factor."

Dancie's gaze narrowed. "How do you even know you've got chemistry?"

"I…just do," she mumbled.

"This is what you warn your clients about!" Dancie leaned back in her chair and threw her hands up. "Falling for the wrong guy and thinking love will magically turn him into the right guy never works out."

"But what if he is the right guy?"

Dancie gasped.

"Calm down. I was speaking hypothetically. You're the one who made the leap from 'intrigued' to 'unhappily ever after.'"

Dancie eyed her for a moment and Piper responded with her bland professional mask. "It's not like I'm going to see him again unless he miraculously changes his mind about taking on a partner and hires me to consult." It was true, and yet she still felt a heavy disappointment. This was not like her.

"Well, good." Dancie didn't sound entirely convinced, because Dancie was her smart, insightful friend. "You were beginning to sound like your mother."

Bringing up her mother was low. "I may have been a little harsh on my mother," Piper said.

Instead of arguing, Dancie looked chagrined. "There's a lot of that going around."

"Really? Tell me." Piper didn't want to talk about Mark Banning anymore. She needed a break from Mark Banning. "You've never had a great lunch with your mother."

"She liked my hair. I told her it was too much trouble and I'd be tempted to cut it all off if it wouldn't look like a fright wig and she told me about the straightening thing." Dancie examined with the ends of her hair. "I can't wait to get this cut."

Piper blinked. "I'm sensing that you're now a pod person."

"No." Dancie dropped her hair. "I unloaded on Mom about this morning. I am so sorry for the way Dad treated you."

Naturally, Piper then thought of Mark. She wished she could get him out of her head. "I wasn't the only one."

"Oh, I know. I'm surprised Mark took it for as long as he did. Travis has freaked out. He's spent the last couple of hours downstairs in the cave throwing a ball against the wall. He won't speak. But never mind about him." Dancie leaned forward, her eyes bright. "Mom told me to quit trying to be a partner in OMG and start my own online business."

"Good for her."

"She said—let me see if I can remember this right—'the way to deal with your father is to go around him, not through him.'"

"I have always liked your mother." Piper brushed at some stray pastry flakes so she wouldn't have to meet Dancie's eyes. She was not proud of feeling sorry for herself because she'd never get useful advice like that from her own mother.

"Well, guess what?" Dancie asked. "She likes you, too, because she offered to invest in the Piper Plan site so we can get started on it right now. I said okay."

Piper's head snapped up. "You want to make The Piper Plan your online business?"

"Well…yeah." Uncertainty crept into Dancie's expression. "It's a great idea and you've done all that research. I mean, I know we'll get way less traffic than if it was a part of OMG, but that will only be for a little while. I've still got my contacts and I've planned some heavy-duty promotion. It's bound to take off." Some of the light went out of her eyes. "I know you could partner with someone else for major bucks, but…I guess I just assumed you'd stick with me."

"Of course!" Piper hastened to reassure her. The software program had been Dancie's idea all along, anyway. "I was just trying to wrap my head around everything."

"So you're okay with it?"

When Piper nodded, Dancie beamed. "Great! Here's what I'm thinking."

Piper helped herself to another croissant. This time, she dipped the end in the mocha cream before taking a bite.

"We spin the dating coach part of your business off on its own site and launch The Piper Plan as part of it." Dancie flipped the laptop around so Piper could see the screen with the website mock-up. "I've talked to the web designer and told him what's up." She pointed to the header incorporating the OMG logo. "This will change. We'll have to reimburse the designer for the work he's already done when I thought the site was going to be part of OMG, but the content will still be usable and he's willing to freelance for us."

Piper let Dancie talk. She was truly happy to see Dancie so enthusiastic, but…Piper felt restless and…trapped. She'd originally hoped that with OMG managing The Piper Plan, she'd become less involved, which Dancie didn't know. Piper couldn't tell her because Dancie would never want to hold Piper back from whatever it was Piper wanted to do with the rest of her life—which was what she'd planned to figure out after today's meeting. "This sounds like a lot of work," she said.

"It is," Dancie agreed. "But I'll be handling the advertising and technical parts so you can concentrate on writing blog posts and being available for phone appointments."

Piper saw the doors of freedom slowly close. "Phone appointments?"

"Oh, I haven't worked out the details, but I figured we would offer a package that included one-on-one time with you." She grinned. "For a price."

And Piper would be paying it. The *trapped* feeling grew. She was going to spend the rest of her life fixing other people's romantic problems without ever having any of her own.

Mark Banning.

Wasn't it interesting how she thought of romantic problems and he popped into her head? Wishful thinking.

Piper reached for the croissants, but Dancie pulled the box across the desk, closed it and set it aside.

"How are you going to find time to do all this?" Piper eyed the box. "What about OMG?"

"Oh, didn't I say? I quit."

"Quit what?"

"OMG. Travis can run the *Women's Guide to Living Fabulous.*" Dancie tossed that off pretty casually for someone who had spent the last two years of college and her entire working career devoted to developing the site. "He wants to be in charge of everything anyway."

Piper felt light-headed. "Give me the croissant box."

"No." Dancie held it away.

Piper lunged.

Dancie was caught off guard and gave up the box. Piper had never eaten three chocolate croissants with mocha cream in a row before. Her teeth sank into flaky, chocolaty goodness. There was a first time for everything.

Dancie watched her. "Is that what I looked like when I stuffed my face?"

Piper mimed crying.

"Worse?"

Piper nodded and took another bite.

"You'll make yourself sick," Dancie told her. "Trust me on this."

She swallowed. "But you quit!"

"I know you think I made a mistake," Dancie said.

Piper knew she'd made a mistake. "I think you were a tad impulsive."

"You overanalyze everything," Dancie told her. "You can't be afraid of making a mistake or you'll never do anything. At least I'm taking action now instead of waiting for a perfect opportunity that might never come."

Is that what Piper did?

Ding ding ding, she imagined she heard as she experienced one of those moments of self-awareness that made her look at her past, present and future in a new way. Child Piper watched her mother make mistakes with men, so adult Piper had actually written a book to show women how to identify and maintain a relationship with their perfect man. And then she made her living fixing other people's relationship mistakes. She, herself, had no mistakes to fix because *she* had no relationships. Romantic ones, at least. Was Dancie right? Maybe Piper wasn't trapped because she felt obligated to Dancie; maybe she was just afraid of making a mistake.

If so, her future looked exactly the same as her present.

Dancie continued to talk, completely unaware that Piper was in the middle of an epiphany.

"The mistake is thinking that Travis and Dad will ever make me a partner, so why waste any more time? This way I'll be able to focus on getting the Piper Plan website up and running. Oh."

"What?" Piper asked, grappling with the fact that Dancie had apparently had an epiphany of her own. Epiphanies must energize Dancie. They just gave Piper a headache.

"Since I quit, I'll have to pack up my stuff pretty quick here." She swiveled the laptop to face her and tapped on the keyboard. "But first, I've got to download my files before they block my password."

"They'd do that?"

"Travis would. It's really lucky that he's nearly comatose right now. Hey—have you got an extra room at your office where I can set up?"

And it just kept getting worse. "No," Piper said firmly.

"That's okay." Dancie wasn't fazed. "I'll squeeze in a corner somewhere until we rent a bigger space. It'll be fun!"

"And cozy." Piper felt a little sick.

"Maybe you could find some boxes somewhere and start packing," Dancie suggested.

Piper rolled her eyes and tossed the half-eaten pastry back into the box. Apparently she could *not* eat three croissants in a row.

Her fingers were greasy. Piper had shoved the wad of napkins she got from the cafe into her purse. As she pulled at one, something flew out with it and clinked onto the desktop.

Mark's locker key.

A sign. She was meant to see him again. Would that be a mistake? Sure! But she was in the mood for a little mistake. She reached for the key.

Naturally, Dancie pounced on it. "'Austin Physical Therapy Center,'" she read from the bright blue plastic ring attached to the end of the key. "And you have this why?"

Piper kept her tone casual. "It's Mark's. I forgot to give it back to him." She held out her hand.

Dancie clutched the key to her chest.

"Hey!"

"Piper, I'm saving you from yourself." She shook her head. "Honestly? I'm disappointed. That's an old trick."

"Really, I just forgot. Remember I told you about getting his pain pills? Come on. Give it back."

Dancie refused. "I think I'll just pop this into the mail."

"That'll take too long." Piper gestured impatiently.

Dancie put the key into the pocket of the khaki blazer she still wore. "I'll let you have it tomorrow."

What happened to taking action and making mistakes? "Why?"

"So your hormones will have time to settle down."

"My hormones are just fine!"

"Obviously," Dancie said. "That's why I'm keeping the key."

She would not be talked out of it, especially when a call to the PT center revealed that Mark's next session wasn't until

Friday. Piper figured that if Mark needed his locker key before then, he'd get in touch.

As the hours passed, she was considerably miffed when he didn't. Okay, so maybe Dancie was right to "save her from herself." In her current frame of mind, who knew what she'd do?

Meanwhile, she spent the rest of the day helping Dancie lug her stuff downstairs and pack it into their cars. The whole time, they never saw Travis, and as far as Piper knew, Dancie hadn't heard from her father.

"Dancie, did you actually tell anyone that you quit?" Piper asked after they'd carried down the last load.

Dancie closed her car trunk. "I emailed everyone who needed to know and shoved a letter under the man-cave door in case Travis isn't reading his email."

"And your dad?"

Dancie shrugged. "Nothing yet."

But the next morning, a giant arrangement of yellow roses arrived at Piper's counseling office. She surveyed the wreck Dancie had made of the tiny reception area. "There's no place to put these."

"Yellow roses. Gotta be from Dad." Dancie plucked out the card and read it as Piper tried to find a flat surface to set the vase on.

"They're for you," Dancie said in a strange voice.

Mark! Mark had sent her roses. How extravagant! Piper buried her nose in one perfect, yellow bloom.

Dancie easily read her. "No, not from Mark."

How embarrassing. "Of course not." Piper tried to bluff her way out. "Why would Mark send me flowers? Besides, exotic flowers would be more his style." She ended up setting the vase on the floor. Dancie handed her the card and turned away.

Thank you. Now find my Dancie a man. B. T. Pollard

Jerk. "Dancie…"

Still with her back to Piper, Dancie held up a hand. Piper's receptionist walked through the door then and Piper had to explain why Dancie's stuff was everywhere. Right after that, her morning clients began arriving, so she didn't get a chance to say anything to Dancie. Not that anything needed to be said. Her father was her father.

The morning was a disaster, at least from Piper's point of view.

As Dancie arranged furniture and chatted with Anna, Piper's receptionist, every sound carried into Piper's consulting room. At least once during each appointment, she had to apologize to her client and get up, open the door and ask Dancie and Anna to keep their voices down.

But then Dancie began making phone calls and she might as well have been right there in the room with Piper.

This was *so* not working. But how could Piper kick Dancie out? Hadn't Dancie taken Piper in when she couldn't afford rent elsewhere?

After hours of being interrupted and tamping down her growing frustration, Piper needed to get away. Returning Mark's key was the perfect excuse. As a bonus, her hormones had definitely gone cold.

She left Dancie and Anna assembling a cheap computer desk Dancie had bought, and headed for the Burns building. Piper had already looked up Mark's office hours and knew he was supposed to be there.

She could have called first, but, well, she didn't want to give him a chance to say something like "Leave it in my faculty mailbox." And she didn't want Dancie overhearing her. It had been difficult enough to wrest the key away from her.

Piper's pulse kicked up a few notches as she opened the door to the Burns building and it wasn't all due to the walk from the parking garage. She was looking forward to seeing Mark again far too much. Even telling herself everything she would have told a too-eager client had no effect.

In the foyer, there was a bulletin board where meeting announcements, roommate requests, items for sale and "rides wanted" were posted. Typical collegiate stuff. But Mark Banning's name on one caught her eye. Piper stopped to read the hand-lettered sign. Mark was advertising for an intern? Seriously? When did he decide to do that? And why? What happened to "I work alone"? Multiple copies of the sign were stuck on doors, trash cans and on the wall by the elevator buttons—places Piper was pretty sure they weren't supposed to be.

Mark's office was on the fifth floor. When Piper stepped into the elevator, she was greeted by yet another copy of his notice. The elevator stopped on the third floor and three girls got in and rode with Piper to the fifth floor. The doors opened and the hallway outside them had more people traffic than Piper had seen in the building so far. She followed the girls and had a feeling she knew where they were going.

Sure enough, they rounded a corner and Piper saw a pile of papers and folders next to one of the doors. That would be Mark's office, she guessed. A piece of paper with his name written in the same handwriting as the notice was taped over the nameplate of the previous occupant. It might say "Mark Banning," but it screamed *temporary*.

Temporary. Piper needed to remember that. Mark was temporary. As in, not sticking around. Just passing time until he was off on his next far-flung assignment.

Piper had wasted enough of her life emotionally investing in temporary men.

She waited until the girls hesitantly added their résumés to the pile outside Mark's *temporary* office, glanced at her and reluctantly left, whispering among themselves.

Under the pile must be the box Mark's notice mentioned. Shaking her head, Piper stepped over the papers that had spilled in front of the door and knocked.

"Leave it outside the door," she heard.

Piper snickered to herself and opened the door. "I don't think you—"

"If you bring that in here, it goes directly into the trash," Mark said without looking up.

Even irritated, the man was a stunner. Cheekbones that could carve a turkey, a manly profile, a thick head of dark hair appealingly mussed in a way that made her want to smooth it from his forehead just to have the excuse to touch him… which she already had. Too bad she'd been in nurse mode at the time and had failed to appreciate the way his body felt against hers. She could appreciate it now. She had a good memory.

In just the few seconds Piper had stood in his doorway, appreciating the memory of Mark's body pressed against hers, her hormones had gone from cold to hot and were dancing in anticipation of making more memories.

Mark sat next to a trash can. As Piper watched, he picked up three résumés, glanced at them and tossed them in. A bulging plastic garbage bag sat next to the bookcase.

Stacks of résumés were on his desk, the chair, the floor beside his desk and in a messy pile just inside the doorway.

Judging by all the applications and the girls she'd seen in the hall, Piper guessed her hormones weren't the only ones doing the happy dance at the thought of Mark Banning.

Maybe she should apply to be his intern. She didn't need two hundred and fifty words to say "Pick me and I'll make it worth your while."

Ugh. She shook her head to clear it and the movement drew his attention. He looked up and for a moment, his expression was blank.

He didn't remember her.

Ouch. Talk about a reality check. Piper was preparing to go into full professional mode and reintroduce herself when Mark's face creased into a breathtaking smile. Literally. Piper had to remind herself to breathe.

While conducting the interviews for *The Piper Plan,* she'd met a lot of good-looking men, most of whom knew it, and she'd always been able to acknowledge their attractiveness without being affected by it. Unless she chose to. Which was rare. The point being, she controlled her emotions; her emotions did not take over and make her stand mutely in doorways, acting like a fan girl.

"Oh—hey." Mark toned down the smile and Piper breathed easier. "You look—" his finger circled next to his face "—different."

That's right. She'd been dressing for BT yesterday. Relief hit her. He hadn't forgotten her after all. "I'm wearing contacts and I ditched the Texas big hair."

"So this is normal you?"

Piper laughed and looked down at her slacks and top. "When I'm seeing clients." Should she have worn something with more pizzazz? No. Anyway, Dancie would have noticed.

She saw his eyes drop to her feet and slowly move upward. "I prefer normal you," he said with a lazy smile.

Piper not only forgot to breathe, she forgot to remind herself to breathe. Only the sound of girlish voices in the hall kick-started her lungs.

Mark groaned. "Quick. Shut the door." When she'd done so, he gestured to the chair. "Excuse the mess. Just shove those onto the floor somewhere."

"I'm not staying." Piper had to force the words out because what she really wanted to say was, "No problem. I'll just sit on your lap."

She knew she was in serious trouble because she was more worried about hurting his leg than how inappropriate sitting on his lap would be.

He'd just boldly checked her out and didn't mind that she could see him checking her out. And Piper, who knew what was going on, still reacted exactly the way he'd known she would. It demonstrated a self-assurance she rarely encountered.

Even worse from her standpoint, was how flattered she felt because he'd bothered. Her body had clearly mutinied.

Time to regain control. She went fishing in her purse. "I forgot to give you your key yesterday."

"I hadn't missed it yet. I've been…" He trailed off and plowed his fingers through his hair.

"I see. What's going on?" Where was the key?

"Applications for an internship—with me." Which Piper already knew. He gave her a chagrined look.

And, yes, it was utterly charming.

By now, Piper was completely disgusted with herself. She felt like two people—one clinically observing and the other mindlessly reacting. She needed to get away from him. Why couldn't she find that stupid key? "What happened to 'I work alone'?"

"Still my preference. But if BT wants me to work with someone, I'll decide who it is. I'd rather train somebody from the start than butt heads with a colleague."

He'd done a complete one-eighty from yesterday. Piper wondered what had changed his mind. His leg? "Did Travis talk you into coming back?"

"I haven't spoken to Travis." Mark watched her search in the bottom of her purse for the key.

This was embarrassing. She picked her way through the papers to the desk and set her purse down. Looking around the small room she said, "These are all applications for being your intern?"

"Yes." He picked up a few from the stack on his desk.

"Since yesterday?"

"Word spread."

"I guess *so*."

He gave her an aw-shucks grin. "What can I say?"

"Ever heard of email?" Piper took out her sunglasses and

set them on the desk, hoping she wouldn't have to empty her entire purse.

"Email is too easy and quick. I figured the extra effort involved in printing out and physically delivering résumés would weed out those who were applying just for the hell of it. Also, I wanted to see who could follow directions." Mark glanced at the top résumé and tossed it into the trash. Same with the next two. He couldn't have spent more than a second reading them.

"Didn't they follow directions?" Piper asked.

"I'm not working with anyone who doesn't know how to spell his or her name. Kourtney with a *K*. Sorry, no. Jenifer with one *n*." He sent another one flying into the trash with a little more force. "And especially not Marc with a *c*. Mark is *M-a-r-k*. Period."

Wow. "What if it's short for Marcus?"

"I don't want to work with a Marcus."

"Well, that's your choice—"

"Yes." Toss, toss. Keep.

"What's that one's name?" Piper asked about the keeper.

"Grace Goodheart." Mark smiled. "Now, that's a name."

"Probably fake."

"Don't care."

Fascinated, Piper watched him quickly dash the dreams of a few more aspiring journalists. Only one résumé caught his attention long enough to scan the second page. Then he tossed it.

"That was Jennifer with two *n*'s,'" Piper said. "What was wrong with hers?"

"She's a freshman. I'm not taking an eighteen-year-old overseas with me."

Piper thought back to the meeting and BT emphasizing that Mark needed someone who could stand up to him. No way would a young intern dare challenge the great Mark Banning. "Your plan won't work, you know."

"Why not?" While she'd been standing there, he'd finished sorting an entire stack and reached for another.

"BT won't agree to a college intern."

"Sure he will. He knows only a complete monster would take stupid risks around a kid."

"They're not kids and you never think your risks are stupid."

He looked up at her. "True."

"He'll still have to approve anyone you take on assignment." And then she heard herself offer, "I can help you with that. When you're ready to interview, I can screen the candidates and tell you which ones BT will find acceptable."

Mark's gaze hardened and Piper realized she should have phrased her offer to emphasize compatibility with Mark and not BT's approval. Oops.

"By the time we leave, I'll have been working with my intern for a couple of months. Why would he disapprove?"

"Because he can," Piper said bluntly. "It's about control and reinforcing his image of himself." And then she quoted the twin's mother. "You've got to go around him, not through him."

Laughing lightly, Mark shook his head and continued plowing through the résumés.

"Actually, hiring an intern is a good strategy," Piper said. "It shows a willingness to compromise on your part—you did not just roll your eyes!"

"Look, Piper." Mark abandoned the papers and sat back in the chair. The fact that his navy crewneck sweater showcased his chest—why hadn't she been paying attention to his chest before?—was a bonus. "I'll admit I was curious about you, so I read a few of your columns."

He'd looked her up? He'd read her columns? Piper's heart thudded and she barely restrained herself from asking what he thought.

No problem. Mark proceeded to tell her. "I'm sure you're

very good at what you do, but there's a lot more involved in choosing an intern than matching up grid squares to find somebody who can make nice with BT."

As a tone of patronization crept into his voice, Piper's heart stopped thudding and beat normally. "Did you go to my website?"

He gave his head a slight shake, his expression telling her he hadn't thought it worth his time.

Her hormones quit dancing and yawned. The tug of attraction she'd felt withered and died, leaving Piper able to acknowledge his looks without being distracted by them, just as always. She was disappointed. "If you had gone to my site, you would know that matching grid squares is an over simplification. There is more to 'what I do' than that."

"Right, right." He rolled the chair behind his desk. "But compatibility is the least important aspect I'll need to consider." He actually looked her right in the eyes as he said it.

"Really."

He didn't seem to be aware that he'd insulted her, which was even more insulting.

"In our business, you meet a lot of people in all sorts of circumstances." Mark settled back in his chair, the very portrait of The Great Man Dispensing Wisdom. "Professionals can't let personalities get in the way of doing their job. The applicants I interview will know that. Personality won't be a factor."

"It's always a factor," Piper insisted. "People can suppress their true nature for only so long. Eventually, it comes out." *Like yours just has.*

Mark regarded her with an expression that incorporated a touch of pity for the mere mortal that she was, along with a condescending smirk. Honestly, it made her want to grab the stacks of résumés from fawning students and fling them at him.

"You have to understand that I'm offering the chance of a

lifetime." He sounded like someone on an infomercial. "An internship with me on a résumé will open any door. It's a career game changer."

How nice that his ego hadn't suffered from being out of the limelight this past year. "Since the position is so important, I would think you'd want to use every resource available to screen your candidates. After all, you and your intern will have to get along with each other, as well."

"It'll be my intern's job to get along with me," Mark stated.

Yeah, the double-alpha arrogance finally made an appearance. "With that attitude, you'll never find someone BT will approve of. But I can."

Piper abandoned her search for the key and unzipped the inner pocket in her purse where she kept her business cards. And there was the key. It figured. Now she recalled putting it in there so she could find it easily.

"Thanks, but no thanks," Mark said just as her fingers closed around his key. "I get that you want to prove yourself to BT. He was pretty harsh." His voice was full of sympathy. Probably faked. "But you'll have to prove yourself with somebody else. This is…bigger than you're used to. The person I take on assignment with me will be operating at the very highest levels of journalism."

Oh, please. Typical alpha, thinking he was the most important thing in the universe.

She'd secretly hoped he was different, but unknowingly, he'd just proved her theories. She was relieved. Truly. She should be running a victory lap. Actually, she should stop wasting time and get out of there.

Withdrawing a business card along with his key, she set them both on the desk. "I hope operating at the very highest levels of journalism doesn't leave your intern too dizzy to do basic research, since you clearly don't have the time."

She turned around and walked out, tossing a "Call me when BT rejects your candidate" over her shoulder.

THAT WAS UNFORTUNATE, Mark thought as he watched her leave. But he'd recognized the expression on her face—a bit dazzled and a lot interested. Ever since he'd become well-known, he frequently encountered that awestruck look on women's faces, especially the young women who signed up for his classes. It was not as wonderful as the *Guys of Texas* readers liked to believe. A man couldn't have a discussion of any depth with a woman who looked at him like that. Their minds were off in a fantasyland of romantic possibilities where he was the star.

A woman looking interested was okay. It was the dazzled part that led to trouble. It was hard to snap them out of it. Being subtle didn't work. Letting them down gently didn't work. Being a jerk was the only thing that did. But that left them angry and no longer interested. And then they'd tell all their friends that he was a jerk.

Mark generally extricated himself before it got to that point.

He was surprised to see the dazzle on Piper's face. It hadn't been there yesterday, but yesterday, he'd been in a world of hurt. Not at his best. Not dazzling. Piper had been the only bright spot in an otherwise awful day. He'd liked that she hadn't been dazzled by him.

Even so, he'd decided she wasn't his type. So when she appeared in his doorway looking exactly like his type, there were a few seconds when he might have looked dazzled, himself.

But not dazzled enough to jeopardize his return to the field. So now she thought he was a jerk.

He looked at the stacks of résumés and 250 word essays on "Why I want to intern with Mark Banning," and knew there were more piling up outside. The intern position had gone viral. Social media. Gotta love it.

Mark pocketed the locker key and picked up Piper's card.

He allowed himself a moment of regret and started to throw it away. He *should* throw it away, but instead he tossed it into his desk drawer.

6

Step six: Get to know your man—and let him get to know you.

PIPER HELD HER HEAD in her hands as shrieks of laughter reverberated through the walls. It had been a week and a half since Dancie commandeered her waiting room. A week and a half of Piper telling Dancie to be quiet, to keep it down, shushing, holding up a hand, miming zipping her lips, reminding Dancie how sound carried through the flimsy walls, knocking on said flimsy walls and even telling her to use her inside voice. Figuring at least once per appointment with a few reminders thrown in between times, it meant Piper had pointed out over fifty times to Dancie that she was too loud. Without effect. Except on Piper's blood pressure.

Worse, Dancie had corrupted the formerly quiet Anna, who now felt free to babble all kinds of opinions that Piper—and her clients—didn't need to hear.

But it wasn't just the noise and the crowded reception area and the lack of privacy. Dancie had started chatting with Piper's clients *and* giving them advice. Yes, trading dating stories, talking about men, *talking about herself.* And since sound carried in both directions, Piper could hear when Dancie contradicted her advice after Dancie clearly eavesdropped on the sessions.

That had prompted a huge fight, their first in…forever.

Dancie got all huffy, which was even worse because it made Piper feel guilty, and then irritated with herself for feeling guilty, and then hyperaware of being overheard, which led to second-guessing herself.

The thing was, after running the *Living Fab* site, Dancie felt she was qualified to give advice. And she was—up to a point. But the clients who sought Piper's help were past that point.

So Piper apologized for overreacting, and Dancie promised to keep quiet. Unfortunately, Dancie's idea of quiet didn't match Piper's.

At least she was able to get out of the office today. Sometimes she needed to see how clients acted on a date, so Piper either set clients up with each other for just that purpose, or observed them on an actual date without their knowledge.

Today, Piper got to play date spy. She loved playing date spy and looked forward to it with an immature glee that probably had a profound psychological meaning she didn't care to explore.

Dancie had once run a piece about spy equipment women could buy online, which had given Piper the idea. She'd bought a purse with a built-in video camera that worked really well and various listening devices that didn't—at least the ones in Piper's price range didn't. That meant she needed to get close enough to the couple to eavesdrop, yet stay far enough away that they didn't see her, otherwise they'd adjust their behavior, which defeated the whole purpose of observing them.

Thus, Piper had acquired a couple of wigs. Okay, maybe more than a couple. It wasn't as though she had a closet full of disguises. Maybe a jacket. A scarf. Sunglasses. Baggy sweatshirt. Hardly anything.

Today, she wore a UT hoodie and a wig with long, straight brown hair. If she took a book and leaned forward to read it, the hair would hide most of her face and she'd look just like any of the thousands of Austin coeds.

"I've never seen you in one of your disguises," Dancie said when Piper emerged from her consultation room.

"I wouldn't call it a disguise. It's just a wig."

"You ought to see her in the ugly gray one," Anna said.

"Is it uglier than that purse?" Dancie made a face.

Piper held it out. "So it's a little large and boxy."

"And plastic," Dancie said. "Why do you have a gray wig?"

"It depends on where I need to blend in." Piper edged toward the door.

"She wears it with a baggy sweater," Anna added.

Anna had a little Dancie hero-worship thing going on. Piper gave her one of those remember-who-pays-your-salary looks.

"Sounds like a disguise to me." Dancie grinned. "Oh, you are enjoying this way too much. I think you missed your calling."

"And what would that calling be?" Piper asked.

"Private investigator, of course."

Piper considered it. "Too depressing. Nobody hires a private investigator to find out something good."

Dancie perked up. "You know…interviewing private investigators would be a great article for *Living Fab*. I should—" She broke off when she remembered she no longer ran the site. "Old habits. Not my problem." She waggled her fingers. "Have fun!"

Piper tried to read her expression for a teensy sign of regret. Nothing. As she left, all she heard was Dancie telling Anna she could take lunch first.

Well, there goes that plan, Piper thought. By now, she'd hoped that Dancie would have regretted her decision to quit OMG, in which case Piper would have groveled to Travis—

even BT—to take Dancie back. But, honestly, she seemed happier than Piper had seen her for months, while Piper was…

Piper was not going to think negative thoughts. It was a beautiful fall day with bright sun, low humidity and a negligible pollen count. She was going to have lunch at Friezen Burger, which served the most insane French fries with hamburger sliders on the side.

Friezen Burger was set up like a diner in a long building with booths marching next to the windows on one side, and bar stools along a counter on the other. Perfect for dating surveillance. Piper sat at the bar where she could position her purse so the camera pointed at the booth behind her.

Toni, the day manager, slid a menu in front of her. "Is another couple finding the road to love too bumpy?"

"I may have to change my disguise," Piper said.

"Then how would I recognize you?" Toni asked.

Piper thought a moment. "You might not. I don't know if I've eaten here as me."

"I don't know, either. That's kinda my point."

They both laughed, and then Toni asked, "You want me to seat the couple in one of those three booths behind you, right?"

"You got it. They should be here in fifteen to twenty minutes." After Piper briefly described the couple, Medina and Vanny, for Toni, she opened the tri-fold menu. It was laminated and slightly slick from the grease-laden air. "I'll need a minute."

"Gotcha. I'll be back." Toni moved off to take another order and Piper happily studied the menu.

The drill at Friezen Burger was to first select the type of potato, Idaho being recommended, and then the cut. It could be sliced or planked or shoestringed or steak fries or fast-food fries or crinkled. Until eating here, Piper had never noticed all the different possibilities. After choosing the cut for the potato, it was on to the type of oil she wanted it fried in. She usually chose peanut oil, but had heard good things about chili oil. However, the chili might be too spicy for the size order she intended to eat. Ever since Dancie started sharing her office, Piper craved yummy carbs, salt and hot fat.

For flavor and crispiness, a girl couldn't go wrong with good ole beef tallow—which was where Piper was in the selection process when her phone vibrated.

She looked at the screen. Travis? She didn't even know Dancie's brother had her cell number. "Piper Scott," she answered, looking around quickly to make sure her couple hadn't arrived yet.

"Hey, Piper. How's it going?"

"Fine. How can I help you, Travis?"

"So you like to cut through the chitchat and get right down to business. I like that."

"I'm working, Travis."

"Yeah, about that."

Great. He was going to cancel her "Dating to Mating" column. She'd half expected it after Dancie had quit OMG.

"I called your office because I was trying to find Dancie and I found her."

"Yes." Friezen Burger was filling up, even though it was early for lunch. Piper pressed the phone to her ear to hear better.

"She really quit."

"Yes, Travis." Piper glanced impatiently at the clock above the cash register.

"I thought she was blowing off steam, but she doesn't want to come back." He sounded surprised.

Piper didn't have time to be diplomatic. "She wanted to be an equal partner and it's clear that you and your dad aren't willing to make her one. So she's moved on."

"Well, good luck to her, then."

Piper's jaw dropped. She would have sworn that Travis was going to ask her to convince Dancie to return.

"Actually, I was calling about something else. Mark Banning. I need a favor."

Well, that got her attention. And she'd done so well not thinking about him. No, she hadn't. The best she'd been able to do was yank her thoughts away when they started wandering in his direction.

"Mark's agreed to come back to OMG and he's even willing to work with someone. But my dad is being a pain in the ass and has rejected everybody Mark has proposed. You said you could find him somebody my dad would approve of, right?"

Incredibly, her heart picked up speed even while her brain countered with memories of Mark's condescension that day in his office. This time, her brain won. "I could if I wanted to. I don't."

"Yeah, Mark said you'd say that."

Was that why Mark hadn't bothered to call her, himself? Conversely, Piper now wanted to prove him wrong, which would mean she'd end up doing what both Travis and Mark wanted. They'd outmaneuvered her and hadn't even been trying.

Toni appeared in front of her. "Decide on those fries, yet?"

Piper shook her head and Toni tapped her watch. "Travis, I've got an appointment in a few minutes. I'm not interested—"

"What would it take? Name it."

Piper started to say that there was nothing that could induce her to work with that jerk, Mark Banning, when she thought of Dancie and the crowded reception area and the fact that Dancie had clearly given Travis Piper's cell number, not that Piper had ever told her, "By the way, Dancie, don't give out my cell number." But Dancie did know Piper was observing clients. Plus, she was countering Piper's advice, and distracting Anna, and was noisy and it was jeopardizing their friendship and… "Dancie gets the use of her old office."

"She doesn't want to come back to OMG," Travis said.

"Not as an employee—just the use of the space."

There was silence. "That's it? That's your price?"

"In addition to my regular fee," Piper told him.

"I knew there was a catch."

"Excuse me—it's how I make my living."

He muffled the phone as he spoke to someone. "Right."

"'Right' as in you agree to let Dancie use her old office?" Piper asked him. Honestly, she'd even waive her fee, if she had to.

"If you come through with somebody for Mark, I'll help her move back, myself," Travis said.

"I'll find someone, but it'll be up to you to convince Mark to work with her." And good luck with that.

"Her?"

"Your dad wanted a female."

"Whatever. I want to get moving on this."

Of course he did. "Please call my office and make an appointment," Piper said evenly, trying and failing to ignore how inconsiderate Travis was being.

Toni caught her eye and Piper saw the couple had arrived a few minutes early. "I have to go, Travis. My clients are here." She ended the call without waiting to hear if he had anything else to say.

So. As she'd predicted, BT hadn't gone for the college intern idea and now Mark was ready to acknowledge that she might just know what she was talking about.

Mark Banning. Part of her went all fluttery at the thought of seeing him again. She didn't like that part, fascinating though it was. Her body was going rogue and there wasn't anything she could do about it. Except ignore it. Which was hard to do. But she would succeed in ignoring it, something her mother never had managed. How did her mother get into her thoughts, anyway? Mark Banning had nothing to do with her mother. Thank goodness.

Toni managed to seat the couple in the booth directly be-hind Piper, so that was working out. She could park her cam-era purse right beside her and get decent video while watching their reflection in the bar mirror. Right now, she could eaves-drop on their conversation, but that would end when the bulk of the lunch crowd arrived.

Piper checked the video feed on her phone to make sure the couple was in the frame, and then opened a notebook to record her first impressions. Their clothes looked fine, the initial seating went okay; he helped her off with her jacket, they both acknowledged their server—Toni—and chatted briefly while looking at the menu. Body language was a lit-tle stiff, but this was a blind date, so she couldn't fault them.

So far, so good. Piper also returned to the menu. She'd de-cided to hang the cholesterol and go for the beef tallow when someone—a male someone—sat on the bar stool next to her.

Something in her responded to this male someone even though she was occupied with the wonderfulness of the fries menu and monitoring the couple behind her.

"A wig. Kinky." His voice dropped. "I like it."

Mark.

Of course.

Everything in her went on full alert. "What are you doing here?" Piper asked, ignoring the fact that he'd recognized her. Dancie strikes again, she suspected.

Mark sat sideways, legs splayed near her thigh, boxing her in, and propped an elbow on the counter. Nothing reserved about that body language, no siree.

"Aren't you wondering how I knew it was you?" He caught a lock of wig hair and skimmed it over his finger.

"No." Piper didn't look up from the menu. Clearly, he was launching a charm assault.

"I recognized your body."

"Encased in the baggy sweatshirt?"

He leaned in close to murmur, "I've got a mind for details and you've got a body worth remembering."

His breath tickled her neck, which caused a chain-reaction tickle all the way down her spine. Piper slapped the menu on the counter. "Seriously? You need a favor and you're going with those lines?"

"They're some of my best." He gave her a cheeky grin that invited her to grin back. Most women probably did and then as easily as that, he was forgiven for whatever he'd done that needed forgiving.

Like insulting her profession.

Even Piper felt her smile muscles twitch, but he wasn't getting off so easily with her. She ignored him as she swiveled her head around so she could catch Toni's eye.

"Here. Let me." Mark straightened and stared in the waitress's direction. And that was all. He just sat up straight and looked Toni's way. And darned if within seconds Toni glanced up from the order she was taking, saw Mark and headed right for him like a homing pigeon. Along the bar, other customers tried to attract her attention just as Piper had, but she had eyes only for Mark.

"What can I get for you?" she breathed as soon as she arrived.

He gave her a classic seducer's smile and drew Piper's menu slowly toward him. "What do you suggest?"

"Ma'am?" called someone fruitlessly.

Toni leaned against the counter, generous cleavage now visible above her black, scoop-necked top. "Anything your heart desires."

"He desires French fries," Piper said. "Because that and sliders are all you serve here."

Without looking away from Toni, Mark matched her body language and leaned in. "I'm interested in what's off the menu."

Toni pursed her lips. "I don't go off-menu until later."

Unbelievable. They were carrying on right in front of her. Toni was cute-guy hardened and Mark wasn't serious, so why did Piper have a problem with it?

Mark closed the menu. "Until then, surprise me."

"You got it." Toni gave him a pretty good seducer smile of her own and glided off to place the order, actually swaying her hips in her expensive and extremely flattering jeans. Mark watched her, which Toni would know because of all the mirrors. She'd know it even without the mirrors.

Her departure launched a chorus of protests including one from Piper. Except Piper's protest was for another reason.

"You are something else," she said to Mark. "Does it always work?"

Mark's gaze lingered on Toni before drifting to her. "What?"

"The charm attack. A couple of smiles, some cheesy flirting and people fall all over themselves to give you what you want?"

"Pretty much." Mark leaned away with a smile Piper wished didn't look quite as self-satisfied as it did.

She also wished she wasn't wearing a cheap wig and baggy clothes, but it was probably best that she was. Cheesy lines and all, her heart was thudding and her skin prickling. And she didn't even like him! She'd have no defenses at all against a bona fide seduction. "Toni didn't take my order."

"We can share," Mark offered, accompanied by a twin of the seducer's smile he'd given Toni.

"Oh, keep your smiles to yourself," Piper grumbled. "And we are definitely sharing."

"I'm willing to share a lot more than fries," Mark responded.

"And the lines just keep coming." Shaking her head, Piper turned away. In doing so, she saw the couple reflected in the mirrored wall behind the bar, the same couple she was supposed to be observing. Mark had distracted her. She made a frustrated sound.

"I didn't say anything."

"Keep it that way. I'm working."

"No, you're not. You're eating lunch."

"I multitask!" Exasperated, her voice rose. She saw the woman behind her glance over. Piper turned her head and let her hair hang forward. "Or I plan to," she said in a quieter voice. "But thanks to you and Travis, I haven't had a chance to order."

"You don't need to order." He pushed the menu away. "We're sharing, remember?"

"I'm very hungry."

He leaned in, his lids heavy. "I like a woman with appetites."

Piper rolled her eyes.

MARK SAW THE EYEROLL. Definitely no dazzle today. He should back up and apologize, but then he'd have to explain that he'd been a jerk on purpose. Then she'd ask why. And there was no way he could tell her he'd done it to get the awestruck look out of her eyes without coming off like a conceited jerk. Since she already thought he was a jerk, it was best to skip the apology and flatter her into helping him.

So far, she'd been immune to his flattery and had retreated behind the impersonal stare he disliked.

He studied her profile. No, he hadn't fooled her, not that he'd sincerely tried. If he was honest, he would have been disappointed if he'd been able to flatter her into helping him after the insulting way he'd rejected her earlier offer.

He'd fooled her then, hadn't he? Mark didn't remember exactly what he'd said, only that he'd kept talking until all the sparkle had left her eyes and her jaw had gone rigid with the effort to remain crisply professional. He'd done it for himself as much as for her, he knew. OMG's Dating Doc had been in his thoughts more than she should have been. He'd looked up her past columns online and heard her voice as he read them. No man bashing. He liked that. She gave a lot of no-nonsense, practical advice with a healthy mix of tough love for the whiners. Lots of reality checks. And she repeatedly cautioned against going into a relationship thinking the other person would change. Smart woman.

A few minutes ago, Mark had stood in the diner's doorway and recognized Piper immediately, even with the wig and the unflattering clothes. That had made him smile, a genuine, pure, from-the-gut smile, just like that day when he'd looked up and discovered her standing in his office doorway.

She got to him and he had no clue why. As he'd walked the length of the diner toward her, he recalled details from their first meeting. His leg had bothered him so much he was surprised that any details had made an impression at all, but it was hard to forget those moments when they'd connected.

Piper Scott wasn't distracted by the Mark Banning fantasy. And in dealing with her, he'd discovered that the Mark Banning personality had no effect on her, either. Unfortunately Mark didn't exactly know how to approach her without one of them.

Be yourself. Oh, sure. Even during those long months with the drug bandits he'd been unable to drop the facade. People liked Mark Banning. They responded to Mark Banning. Regular old Mark was forgettable.

He needed a different approach. Right now, Piper was more interested in people-watching in the bar's mirrored backsplash than she was him.

She pushed her hair out of the way and sipped her water. It was interesting how the dark wig made her skin look whiter. It was probably white all over.

And just like that, an image of Piper naked popped into his mind. He had an instant, visceral zero-to-sixty reaction before banishing the imaginary Piper so fast, he didn't know if she'd been wearing the wig in his fantasy or not.

The aftereffects lingered. And lingered. Mark concentrated

on her profile and told himself he would have reacted to the image of any naked female, because his body was healing. Had healed. In fact it was in prime condition.

He should check his any-naked-female theory soon. Correction: any-naked-female-but-Piper theory. Getting naked with Piper would be bad. *Great.* Wrong. *Oh, so very right.* He had to convince her to work with him. *What better way than—*

"You're staring at me," she said.

He was doing way more than that. "You have a pretty nose." And that was pure Mark speaking. Pure Mark had no experience with women, obviously.

She gave him a sideways glance. "I have a pretty nose?"

"Yes. It's…strong." Pure Mark should shut up.

"Have you ever considered that your lines are so bad, women do what you want so you'll stop saying them?" she asked.

"Whatever works."

"An apology would work."

Mark thought about it. "Too soon. I haven't been proven wrong, yet. But I'm willing to give you a shot at it."

She smothered a laugh. "Is that supposed to motivate me?"

"Actually, yes."

Not only didn't she react, she wasn't even looking at him.

"Think how you'll feel when I have to admit that I was wrong to ignore your advice," he said.

"You were wrong." She opened a small writing pad and clicked her pen. "It doesn't matter to me if you admit it or not."

Wow. Looks like he should have gone for the apology. Too late. If he did so now, she wouldn't believe him.

He saw her write *hand-cheek, slouch* and he found himself automatically straightening. His leg was beginning to twinge, anyway. "BT called your work fluff. Now I *know* you want to prove him wrong. Here's your chance."

He heard her take a slow breath and knew he had her. "So? Are you motivated?"

Staring straight ahead, Piper sighed. "I can't believe Dancie told you where I was."

"She didn't. Travis recognized the background noise." He looked around. "I've heard about this place but I never managed to eat here."

"Did Travis also mention that I asked you to make an appointment?"

Wait—was he behind the curve? "You mean you already agreed to work with me?"

She made a small sound. "Travis and I came to terms— doesn't anyone listen to what I say anymore?"

"I may have left before you two got to that part." Mark had been out of the *Guys of Texas* office as soon as Travis told him where she was.

She turned slightly, but without taking her eyes away from the mirrored blacksplash behind the serving bar. "This is an example of the impulsiveness that gets you into trouble."

"Am I in trouble?"

She took a minute to think about it. "No, but only because I'd made a deal with Travis before you got here. Otherwise, I would have told you to get lost."

Smiling, he swiveled the bar stool and leaned sideways against the counter. "But you didn't."

"I am now. Get lost. Make an appointment."

"Why? I'm already here. I've got fries coming."

She glanced at him. "There is that. But I can't discuss your situation now. I'm *working.*"

Mark followed her gaze to the mirror. Belatedly, he realized she was actively observing someone and not just people-watching. "Are you spying on the people behind us?"

"Shh."

"So that's why you're wearing the wig." Mark watched them for a few seconds. "What's their story?"

"Nice people with problems getting second dates. I'm trying to find out why."

No glaring reason stood out to Mark. The girl was low-key pretty. She could stand to sex it up, but then again, it was the middle of the day and they were in a diner that served fries. "Blind date?" he asked.

"Uh-huh." Piper sounded distracted and she was squinting.

"And he takes her to a crowded place that only serves one thing?"

"Two things. Fries and sliders."

"Still."

Her lips curved. "You'll understand when you taste the fries."

Piper's profile was to him and her sexy half smile caught him off guard. Off guard as in he took another unexpected zinger to the gut. And he wasn't even thinking about her naked.

His mouth went a little dry. That was a smile of remembered pleasure, that's what it was. If she smiled that way when she thought about food, how would she look when she remembered other pleasures?

Suddenly, other pleasures became very important to Mark. He remembered those pleasures. Barely. He needed a refresher. Gazing at Piper speculatively, he wondered if anyone had refreshed her memory lately. For some reason, no doubt completely self-serving, he thought not. She didn't come across as repressed. No, she was more like paused and waiting.

He gazed straight ahead the way she was, but he was looking at her in the mirror and not at the couple behind them.

He didn't think she noticed. He *hoped* she didn't notice, because when his gaze shifted to his face, he saw desire reflected back at him. Desire to refresh her memory and his own, and then make new memories, the kind that would bring that intriguing half smile to her face when she thought about them.

His body was definitely healing, because he hadn't had an attack of sudden desire like this in ages. It was the way his encounters with women usually played out. An opportunity or a tense situation led to desire flaring and they acted on it. Each knew it was a pleasure of the moment. Not that there couldn't be several moments, or days, but when real life intruded, the flare just as quickly burned out. It was fun while it lasted, but it couldn't last long, and he and the woman both wanted it that way.

He didn't know what Piper wanted, except that she didn't want him. He'd made sure of that. Absolutely no dazzle remained in her expression.

She did not like him, not that it was necessary for her to. But he sensed she didn't dislike him, either. No, this was much worse. Apathy.

It was rare for Mark to find himself at a loss the way he was now. People either loved him or hated him, but they were never indifferent.

Let it go, he told himself. The important point was that she'd agreed to evaluate applicants for him. *Tell her thanks and go make the appointment.*

He was about to when Piper made another one of her notes: *12:23—initiate, make more of an effort to engage.* So she liked action. Good to know, because action was Mark's specialty.

7

Step seven: Look for signs that he's amenable to a relationship. Pay particular attention to the way he treats women and the way they treat him.

Whipping out his phone and Piper's business card, Mark tapped in her number. "I'm calling for an appointment," he told the female who answered. It sounded like Travis's sister. "It's Mark Banning."

"Oh, hi, Mark. This is Dancie. How's it going?"

"Great. Especially if she has an opening this afternoon." At the last minute, he remembered to avoid saying Piper's name aloud.

Their eyes met in the mirror. He gave her a slight nod to reassure her that he would be careful not to let the couple behind them overhear. He'd been in similar situations many times before.

"Doubtful," he heard Dancie say. "She stays pretty booked. You'll need to talk with her receptionist, but she's at lunch. Can I have Anna call you?"

"Please." After leaving his number, he asked, "Dancie, could you do me a favor and check her schedule? If today is a possibility, I'll need to do some juggling."

When he said Dancie's name, Piper blinked. It wasn't much of a reaction, but it was something. Better than that clinical stare.

"If today is a possibility, Anna will be the one to tell you," Dancie snapped.

This time, Mark blinked. "Hey, I figured it was worth a shot. Thanks." He disconnected. "Your receptionist is going to call me," he told Piper.

She was back to watching the couple. "Good."

Seconds later her phone buzzed with an incoming text. Glancing down, she smiled as she read it. "Apparently you're pushy."

"It's how I make things happen," he said as she tapped a response. "Because I'm an action kind of guy."

Piper pressed "send." She didn't comment about him being an action kind of guy.

"What did you say?" he asked her.

"I told Dancie to push back." She set the phone down.

"Great. Now I won't get in for weeks."

"Didn't your mother teach you to take turns?"

"My mother wasn't around enough to teach me much of anything." It just slipped out and he wished it hadn't.

Piper turned her head and faced him fully, the first time she'd done so since he'd tracked her down at the restaurant. They locked eyes. *There's your way in,* instinct told him.

He ignored it. "Relax. I'm not going to play the poor, motherless boy card." Unfortunately he couldn't play the seducer card, either, and that was his best card.

"*Were* you a poor, motherless boy?"

"No. Mom was a single parent in the military. I got bounced around to relatives and friends, and then friends of relatives, and on occasion friends of friends. And once the neighbor of a friend of a friend."

Her expression changed and he knew she was analyzing this new data. He didn't like being analyzed, so he'd thrown in that last bit. But when she inhaled sharply and gave him an appalled look, he decided he didn't like that, either. "She had car trouble. It was only for a couple of hours. I made it sound worse than it was."

"Why?"

"To get a reaction from you!" How did she get him to admit this stuff? "You have this way of staring at me without any expression and I imagine your mind collecting and sorting data so you can fit me in one of your little squares. And it bugs the hell out of me." There.

"You went to my website!" She beamed.

It figured *that* would be the thing that pleased her. "Yes, I went to your website." He'd expected to find more about dating. "I wouldn't be here if I didn't think you could help."

"Excellent." She looked pleased with herself as she checked on her dating couple. "So—was any of what you said true?"

"All of it." The words shot out like bullets propelled by years of bitterness.

She raised her eyebrows.

Yeah, he still had issues, but why was he getting all worked up about it now? Looking over her shoulder, he fixed his gaze on the serving window as basket after basket of fries appeared. "Sorry. I don't go around telling people about my childhood traumas."

"It explains a few personality traits and it would have come out in the compatibility interview, anyway." The matter-of-fact way she spoke helped him contain the emotional overflow.

"What about your dad?"

He figured she'd ask sooner or later. "Not in the picture. He and my mom served together. When she told him she was pregnant, he told her he was married. End of story."

She nodded. "Did you ever meet him?"

"Not in person." Mark was losing his appetite and had no one to blame but himself. She'd told him she didn't want to discuss his situation now and he should have listened. "I contacted him, but he wouldn't see me without a DNA test. I refused. But last year when I was the flavor of the month, he got in touch."

"And you refused to see him without a DNA test."

He glanced at her. "Too predictable?"

"Just expected. He hurt you and you wanted to hurt him back. A lot of people would react the same way."

"Would you?"

Slowly, she shook her head. "Only because I want to see what he looks like."

She wasn't speaking hypothetically. "You don't know what your father looks like?" he asked softly, sliding in the question. Maybe she'd forget they were discussing him.

"I thought I did. I spent my whole childhood being angry at the man I'd thought was my dad, who left when I was little. But when I started asking Mom questions so I could track him down on the internet, she told me that my real father had abandoned us when I was a baby. Lucky me. Abandoned twice."

Now, there was a piece of insight, Mark thought. "So we both grew up without fathers."

"I had way too many fathers, but yes, we have that in common. Congratulations. Now we've bonded."

The dry way she spoke made him laugh. His phone buzzed just then and it was her office calling.

"Banning," he answered. He listened a few moments and muted the phone. "You're solidly booked for at least a month."

Without looking at him, she held out her hand and he gave her his phone.

"Anna, how much red time did I block out this afternoon?" After a second, she said, "Okay. I'll be seeing Mark Banning within that block. Sure." She handed him back his phone.

Excellent. "I appreciate it. What's red time?" It was odd to keep speaking to her profile.

"Research. I've got a corporate consultation at three. I like color-coding my calendar," she offered. "That way I can see how my day will be at a glance. Purple means an in-person appointment, green means I go out, black means I'm unavailable. Blue means break." She was making notes as she spoke.

"Thanks," he said.

"No problem. I did offer."

"Not about that—for what you're doing now."

"Mmm?" She frowned, but it was because of something she saw in the mirror.

"You revealed something about yourself so I wouldn't feel awkward about oversharing. And you did it while observing your other clients whose appointment I crashed." He leaned back and shook his head. "Believe it or not, I'm usually a lot smoother than this."

"Oh, I believe it."

He laughed softly. He thought about leaving so she could finish up with the couple undisturbed. On the other hand, the sooner their problems were solved, the sooner Piper could start finding him a handler.

Turning his attention to the couple, Mark observed the guy in the mirror. He slouched in the booth and fingered the packets of artificial sweetener in their little ceramic holder. He wore jeans and a T-shirt with a windbreaker bunched on the seat beside him. He was probably trying to look casual cool but was coming off as disinterested.

The girl smiled determinedly and lobbed conversational starters at him, which he would answer before lapsing into silence. Then she'd take a sip of her drink and try again. The only time he perked up was when their food arrived. The server set two oval plates mounded with French fries in front of them, along with a circular holder filled with tiny cups.

"What's that metal thing?" Mark asked.

"Dipping sauces."

He watched as the girl repositoned her plate, lined up her fork and used a napkin to wipe away the condensation from her glass. Then she pulled the holder until it was directly in the center of the table, checked, and nudged it a bit to one side.

"Mmm." Piper made a note.

"That's what I was thinking."

"Shh." Piper had leaned forward, squinting even more, her lips moving slightly.

Mark's attention was caught by her lips—fuller than he remembered from the sexy half smile earlier. Nice pouty lips wasted on a woman who wasn't the pouty type. If she were... He inhaled sharply as his imagination went a little crazy. Again.

"What?" Piper asked.

Mark grappled for something to say. "Nobody's dipping."

He wasn't looking at her or her pouty lips as he spoke, but felt her study him silently for a few seconds before checking out the couple again.

"They're talking about the sauces, though. He recommended one."

"If the fries are so great, then how come neither one has eaten any yet?" As Mark spoke, the girl tentatively took a fat fry and gingerly dipped it in a mustard-colored sauce.

"Big test coming up," Piper murmured. "No double dipping."

The guy took one of his fries and dipped it in the same sauce. "He chose the same flavor. Does that have some psychological significance?" Mark was being sarcastic, but Piper answered him seriously. At least he thought it was seriously.

"He's mirroring. When you find someone attractive, you match their body language and expressions."

Mark knew about mirroring, but he didn't think it applied here.

Piper stared intently. "I wish I could make out what they're saying and why she's holding that French fry like it's going to bite her."

"He told her the mustard is his favorite and she said she's

not much of a mustard fan and he said it wasn't ordinary mustard and she should try it."

She glanced at him. "You read lips?"

His gaze dropped to her mouth. "It comes in handy."

"I wish I was better at it," Piper said as the guy stuffed the whole fry in his mouth.

"Mmm," she said, and scribbled one of her notes. She said *mmm* a lot and he sensed it wasn't positive.

Mark was about to tell Piper that he'd figured out the guy's problem when the girl took a huge bite of her fry—would that be mirroring? As they watched, her eyes got huge, she coughed and grabbed for her water. "Hot Chinese mustard I'm guessing?"

"It's on the menu, but I've never had it," Piper said. "And now I don't think I ever will."

The girl dabbed at her eyes and fanned her face.

"You're kidding," Mark said when the guy hid a smile. "Did you see that?"

"Yes."

"I expected you to sound more outraged."

"I've seen worse."

The poor girl had barely recovered when her date did the strangest thing—he moved the sauce server a little to one side and nudged her drink glass. Then he ate a fry off her plate and sat back. Sniffing, the girl repositioned the sauce server and her glass and arranged her fries to fill the hole left by the one he'd snitched. Fascinating. But wasting time.

"Well, I think we've identified the problem here," Mark said.

"Have we?"

"Oh, come on. She's a little OCD and he's a jerk."

Piper continued to watch the couple, but it was obvious to Mark that this was the first and last date for these two. "That guy totally isn't into her. So now what?"

Before Piper could answer, Mark caught sight of their

server bearing down on them with a huge platter of fries and two of the sauce holders hooked over her arm.

"It's the Friezen prize platter," Piper said with awe in her voice as a mountain of fries appeared in front of him. "Wow, Toni."

The server, who was eyeing Mark with exactly the kind of direct, uncomplicated interest he liked, glanced at Piper.

"Oh." Blinking, Toni straightened. "Piper, you should have waved me over. Are you ready to order now?"

Piper brought her finger to her lips. "Sorry," Toni mouthed with a glance at the couple.

"Mark and I are sharing," Piper said, making it sound like so much more.

That was interesting.

Toni's smile grew brittle as she looked from one to the other drawing exactly the conclusion Piper wanted her to. She dumped a handful of extra napkins next to the sauces. "Enjoy."

This time, there was no sway in her walk as she moved down the bar.

"Was that nice?" Mark asked mildly.

"You'll leave her a big tip to make up for it."

"Is that what my type does?"

She took a plank-style fry and dipped it into a creamy sauce. "Along with ninety percent of the other types." She took a bite. "Mmm." And it was an entirely different *mmm* from her critical *mmm*s. It was a moany little *mmm* and definitely meant *good*. Mark would bet French fries weren't the only thing that elicited a moany little *mmm*.

"Béarnaise sauce. I never wanted to waste one of my choices on the béarnaise." She stared at the half-eaten fry in her hand. "Now, why didn't I think I would like it?"

Mark tried some. Yeah. Definitely moanworthy. He'd tasted three more combinations before he realized that the past few minutes, he'd been thinking about nothing but the taste of the French fries. Hot and crisp, just the right amount of salt. Great naked, even.

Just then, Piper gave another of her little *mmm*s so it was inevitable that his next thought would be that Piper would be great naked. He couldn't keep having these thoughts about her, at least not right now while she was sitting next to him moaning and licking her lips. Her full, pouty lips.

Warning. Disengage.

He set down the matchstick potatoes he'd been dipping in the peanut sauce. He drew two deep breaths. He sipped his water.

Then he listened to the sound effects from Piper and knew he was in trouble if he didn't put physical distance between them.

Piper hadn't looked at the couple behind them since the fries arrived, so Mark checked on them for her.

"Hey. The lovebirds aren't doing so well."

Guilty surprise flashed across her face and she swiveled to look in the mirror.

Everything on the couple's table had been set in strict lines. As they watched, the girl finished arranging all the fries on her platter parallel to each other. By length.

"Uh-oh," Piper said. "It always takes a long time to get over stress-induced—"

"You know, she's not the only one with a problem." Mark threw down his napkin and slid off the stool. "I can fix this."

"Mark!"

He ignored Piper's angry whisper. Why waste time when he could just show these two what they were doing wrong? "I only need a couple of minutes tops," he promised Piper.

"Mark!" She reached for his arm, but he pulled away.

"Relax and watch how it's done."

IF SHE HADN'T BEEN DISTRACTED by the most wonderful fries in the universe, she would have predicted something like this. Too bad she'd been using the fries to distract her from Mark, who had very cleverly revealed deeply private emotions about his childhood, which had prompted a few revelations of her own. Only, she knew he hadn't been clever on purpose. She wished he had been. She really did. It would be so much easier to dislike him for trying to manipulate her. And she needed to dislike him to remain emotionally detached. Negative plus positive equaled safe. Neutral plus positive meant trouble.

Speaking of trouble, she couldn't stop Mark from interfering with her couple without drawing attention to herself. And maybe she wouldn't have stopped him even if she could. *It's how I make things happen,* he'd said. Here was the famous Mark Banning impulsiveness in action and she had a ringside seat.

Besides, she had all these fries sitting in front of her. Wouldn't want them to get cold.

Mark turned on the charm—maybe a bit too much judging by the deer-in-the-headlights look from her couple.

Wow. What a smile. Were those dimples? She hadn't noticed dimples before. These weren't cheerleader-cute dimples, either. These were manly dimples. She didn't know manly dimples existed, but Mark sure had them. Piper mindlessly grabbed from the platter and without looking, jabbed her fries into the nearest sauce. Was it possible to dimple at will? To have dimples only when you wanted? Was there some kind of dimple muscle you could exercise?

Dimples were very appealing, Piper decided, helping herself to another grease-laden potato.

Mark put his hand on Vanny's shoulder and a moment later, they'd changed places. Mark gracefully slid into the booth.

Slick. *He's slick,* Piper thought. *I should remember that. I don't like slick people.*

And then she registered the taste in her mouth and grimaced. Curry. Not a fan. Searching among the sauces, she plucked out the little cup of golden sauce and set it aside.

"You see how I'm sitting," she heard Mark say. Everyone within twenty feet could hear him.

Piper went for a reddish sauce. Cajun with a nice bite. Appropriate because she was feeling like she wanted to bite somebody. Somebody like Mark.

"Positioning your body like this tells her you're interested. Sitting like this—" and he slouched in an excellent imitation of Vanny's posture "—says you'd rather be somewhere else."

"Uh, sir?" Vanny protested.

"Just watch and learn." Mark leaned forward in the "interested" position he'd demonstrated.

Piper and Vanny watched Mark charm—that word again—Medina. He swept away the silly barrier of condiments she'd built and she didn't try to line them up again. He plucked fries from her carefully arranged platter, destroying the order. She didn't notice.

He chatted—probably wittily. His eyes stayed on her—probably appreciatively. He laughed and it even sounded genuine. Then he said something—probably an outrageous compliment.

Medina's cheeks pinkened and she touched her hair.

Exhaling, Piper selected fries with salsa. Mark had some serious moves. It was a little frightening.

Medina asked him something and Mark launched into a lengthy answer. Piper had no idea what the topic was, but Mark had leaned forward and was gesturing with his hands the way he did when he really believed in what he was saying. She'd noticed it at the meeting and during his lecture. He projected an attractive intensity without become preachy or arrogantly pompous.

Funny how that day in his office he'd come across as both.

While he spoke with her, Medina's entire body rearranged itself without seeming to move. Her muscles visibly relaxed, her shoulders tilted, and her hands stopped their nervous clenching and unclenching.

"That's better," Piper heard him say. "You look much more relaxed and so I feel relaxed." He paused, smiled and held her gaze for at least four counts. "Relaxed is very attractive."

Holy cow. Piper swallowed. Did any female stand a chance of resisting him?

Mark took one of Medina's fries and dipped it into plain, old ketchup. "Ready for some fun?"

Medina nodded and Mark offered her the fry. When she reached for it, he held the fry away. "You want me to feed you."

"I do?"

"You do. Lean forward."

"Seriously?" Piper murmured as Medina leaned toward Mark with her mouth open.

"First lean, then open," he said.

"Can I have a do-over?" Medina asked.

"Absolutely." Mark held out the fry and Piper found herself mindlessly eating from the platter.

Medina gave a little shoulder shake in preparation and then locked eyes with Mark. Slowly, she leaned forward.

"That's it," Mark encouraged her. "Now what you want to do here is bump your lip against the sauce."

Medina bumped and immediately grabbed for a napkin leaving Mark still holding a French fry above the middle of the table. And he didn't look ridiculous doing it.

"The bump was good," he told her. "Very realistic and natural. The whole idea is to lick the sauce off."

Medina looked uncertainly at him. "The French fry?"

He smiled patiently. "Your lips."

Piper's tingled as he spoke.

Medina leaned forward and smiled appealingly as the fry touched her mouth. Medina was a very fast learner.

"Good. Now lick it off—too fast." He bumped her lip again. "Lick it off slowly, but not porn-star slowly."

"What's porn-star slowly?" she asked.

"Never mind. Just don't exaggerate. Yes," he said after Medina's second attempt. "That's good."

"Now what?" she asked.

"Open your mouth a little and nibble the fry in."

It looked totally contrived to Piper, but Vanny seemed fascinated.

"Now you feed me," Mark instructed. He threw a glance toward Vanny. "Pay attention."

"I am *so* paying attention," Vanny assured him.

Giggling, Medina picked up a fry and offered it to Mark.

He closed his hand over her wrist, holding it in place. Gazing into her eyes, he slowly ate the fry and when it was gone, he drew a couple of her fingers into his mouth.

"Whoa," Vanny mouthed.

No way, Piper thought. That was the corniest thing she'd ever seen. And yet, her fingertips tingled and she swore she felt Mark's tongue on them. She *wanted* to feel Mark's tongue on them. She wanted to feel Mark's tongue *everywhere*.

Medina stared unblinking as Mark nibbled and did who knows what to her fingers.

This had to stop. The young men Medina dated would never act this way. They couldn't pull it off.

But it worked for Mark. Deliberately looking away, Piper grabbed for the paper napkins and wiped her hands. She was finished with fries forever. How could she ever eat them without thinking of Mark?

When she looked again, Medina had a gooey expression on her face—wide, unblinking eyes, slack jaw, parted lips. Piper knew how she felt. *And I'll bet I looked exactly the same way that day in his office.*

With a jolt she felt all the way to her stomach, she realized Mark got that you're-so-handsome-I-can't-breathe expression a lot. He'd seen it on her face, too.

"Are you single?" Medina asked. Piper read her lips clearly.

So did Vanny. "Hey, now. Have you forgotten that you're on a date with me?"

"Yes," Medina said.

Mark smiled, maybe even chuckled, his head ducking modestly. "I'm flattered," he told Medina, which Piper could have predicted. He said something else she couldn't make out and as he did so, he straightened, withdrawing his hands from the table and moving them out of sight. When he finished letting Medina down, his smile was kind, not sexy, and it certainly wasn't one of his killer charming ones. Very nicely done.

But something about the scene and his posture looked familiar to Piper. Though Mark was very clearly withdrawing, Medina couldn't see it. She actually scooted forward until the edge of the table pressed into her midriff. Piper wasn't sure what she was saying, but she said it with an eager desperation that was uncomfortable to witness.

Piper was about to intervene when Mark slouched against the back of the booth and Piper got another shock of recognition. It was his office chair pose. He was going through the same withdrawing and increasingly insolent body-language routine as he had with Piper.

Her face flamed—she saw it in the mirror. She felt a little sick and a lot embarrassed.

He spoke and whatever he said to Medina had her blinking as though she'd come out of a trance. Piper remembered feeling that way, too.

"Okay. That's enough." Vanny tapped Mark on the shoulder.

When they'd switched places and Vanny sat in the booth again, Medina actually smiled at him. Clearly, she'd recovered from the Mark Banning enchantment faster than Piper had, finger licking and all.

How could she work with him now?

Piper spent a few moments trying to come up with a plausible explanation for reneging on her deal with Travis and then she got mad. Why was she embarrassed? She'd returned his key and he'd totally misread her. She'd been doing him a favor, not flinging herself at him. He was the one who should be embarrassed for thinking he was so incredibly attractive that she wouldn't be able to control herself in his presence. And the offer to help was only because BT had suggested it first.

He'd completely overreacted. Piper wasn't denying that'd she'd—briefly—found him attractive, but she hadn't imagined the interest on his part, either. And no, she was not counting his heavy-handed flirting today. She remembered those moments when they'd looked into each other's eyes and the way he'd smiled when he'd recognized her.

And then he'd spoiled it all, which made her angry all over again. Good. She'd use her anger as a shield. Mark was now her client, so they'd be working together. She had no doubt he'd try to charm her and any woman he hired into doing what he wanted. It was automatic with him.

That was going to stop. He didn't get to flirt and smile and lick fingers, and then smack women down when they responded. She thought of Medina's face and what her own must have looked like, and shuddered.

Right then, Piper vowed that never again would Mark Banning put that expression on her face.

8

*Step eight: Do you have chemistry together? Now's the
time to find out.*

SHE WAS GONE. IN THE FEW minutes the guy had blocked Mark's
view of the bar seating, Piper had packed up her stuff and
walked out. She'd left behind a whole lot of fries, too.

Mark popped a couple into his mouth as he tossed enough
money onto the counter to cover whatever he owed and a
tip that would land somewhere between generous and truly
memorable.

Then he took off after Piper. He guessed she was ticked
off or she would have hung around to thank him. Or at least
to finish the fries. But they were cold now, anyway.

He spotted her a block ahead and launched into an un-
gainly hopping jog. "Hey, Piper! Wait up!"

She kept walking.

Mark slowed to a walk. If she wasn't going to talk to him,
he wasn't going to risk his leg. "We have an appointment!"
he called after her.

She whipped around and glared until he caught up. "At my
office. Where I am going." The fall breeze caught strands of
the wig and she brushed it impatiently away from her face.

Mark stared at her mouth, remembering the half smile. He'd like to see it from this angle. No chance of that now. "You're mad."

"Yes."

She continued walking, but at a slower pace, which irritated him. Irrationally, but it did.

"Don't slow down on my account."

She sped up and he knew he'd pay later. "All right, yes, do slow down on my account."

She did. "Do you ever think before you speak or act? Or do you always just start right in and figure stuff out as you go along?"

"You snooze, you lose," he said.

"When you're sleep-deprived, you make mistakes," she countered.

"Better imperfect than nothing" was his response. He'd had discussions like this before.

Piper's steps slowed even more and she had the strangest expression on her face. "You're right."

Which was not what he'd expected her to say.

Then she picked up the pace and her tone hardened. "But not always. Sometimes nothing is better than a bad something."

Mark didn't know what "something" she referred to, but he guessed it wasn't about him. "Are you mad that I sped things along with the couple? I know you worked me in this afternoon, so I thought if I helped you with them, it would save time."

"You interfered. In your usual self-centered, arrogant, conceited way, you assumed you knew more about my subject than I do."

"It's *dating*." He gave her a you've-got-to-be-kidding-me smile.

"Do you go on many dates?"

Actually, he did not. "I don't have much downtime when I'm in the field."

"So that's a 'no' to dating a lot."

Why was she making such a big deal out of this? "Well, not the whole flowers and dressing up and expensive restaurant routine, but I've got no problems with the ladies."

"Of course you don't." Her clinical voice matched her clinical expression and he disliked both. "They flock to you. Thick crowds of women surround you, jaws slack, their glazed eyes following your every move, ever hopeful that you'll deign to shine the bright light of your devastating smile upon them."

"Piper."

"Then you crook your finger and the lucky lady follows you into your lair, eager to do your bidding until you tire of her."

"Piper!" He stopped and grasped her arm, turning her so they faced each other.

Angry brown eyes glared up at him and he promptly forgot what he'd been going to say.

Awareness flowed through him. Traffic noises receded and he ignored the pedestrians walking around them while they stood right in the middle of the sidewalk next to a live oak tree.

Those eyes of hers were going to get him into trouble. They saw right through to the man behind the facade. No one else had ever thought to look, not that Mark stuck around long enough to give anybody a chance.

It was unnerving the way she was able to strip all emotion out of her face and voice so he never knew what she was thinking. The most her eyes had ever expressed was a detached curiosity.

Until now.

She was furious with him. Sure, she wore the same detached expression, but her eyes were angry. So very angry. Other than a brief flash of pity, it was the only strong emotion he'd provoked in her. At least she felt something for him. It didn't matter that it was anger and not desire. Passion was passion, no matter what the emotion. If Piper could feel anger, she could feel desire. Mark already felt desire.

If she were someone else and they were someplace else, Mark would demonstrate just how quickly anger could become desire. The cause of her anger wouldn't matter because when the passion disappeared, so would he. It would be simple and uncomplicated, and they'd both be left with terrific memories.

But they were not someplace else and Piper was the woman who connected with the Mark Banning other women never saw, so it did matter what made her angry.

He'd have to deal with it. Mark wasn't good at dealing with deep emotions, at least other people's deep emotions, yet he knew interfering back at the diner wasn't enough to make her this angry at him. There was something more. But what?

The muscles in her arm bunched, reminding him he still had his hand wrapped around it. An instant later, she jerked away.

"What?" She practically snarled the word.

"I'm sorry if I made you angry," he said, taking care to inject sincerity into his voice.

"If you made me angry? You're not sure?"

"Yes. I'm sure. I'm very sure I made you angry. And I am sincerely, truly, deeply sorry."

"What are you sincerely, truly, deeply sorry for?"

"Making you angry." This was going even worse than he'd expected.

"Yes, but how did you make me angry?"

"Do apologies come with quizzes now?" Mark was getting a little angry, himself.

"An apology is an expression of regret, Mark. You can't regret something if you don't know what it is."

"I'm beginning to regret apologizing."

She shook her head and started walking again. "You barged into my business without thinking, without considering the consequences."

He'd thought the consequences would be getting the couple back on track faster so she'd have more time for him. "I was trying to help. The guy needed a few tips and I thought he'd take it better from me than from you."

"The idea was for me to observe a typical date. What you did is not typical. If they'd been a random couple you noticed in a restaurant, would you really have approached the guy and critiqued him in front of his date?"

"No, but they weren't a random couple."

"That's not the point." Piper took a long slow breath and let it out just as slowly. "You interfered when I asked you not to. That's the point."

Mark thought. "I don't recall you telling me not to interfere."

"You didn't give me the chance." She gazed steadily at him. "I think you do that all the time. You just start doing something and ignore or pretend not to hear anyone else's opinion."

For a few beats, Mark looked down the street. She was right, but most of the time people were only going to try to talk him out of something he was going to do anyway. Or they had nothing of value to add and just wasted his time.

He looked back at Piper. "Because in the time people spend yammering about something, I can get it done."

"Even if it's wrong?"

"Then at least you've got something to fix."

"Back at Friezen's?" She gestured behind them. "There was nothing that needed to be fixed."

Difference of opinion. "I'm sorry I interfered. But you saw how that girl was reacting—why did you let it go on so long?"

"I was videotaping them."

"Where's the camera?" Mark looked her over. "In the ugly purse?"

Piper drew it closer to her. "Why does everyone think this purse is ugly?"

"Because it is?"

She gave him an irritated look and started walking.

"Look. I'm sorry I messed things up for you. Now are we good?"

She put a hand on his forearm. Her touch startled him and he stopped abruptly to look down at her.

She moved around to stand in front of him on the sidewalk, her eyes still intense, but no longer angry. "Don't ignore me ever again."

"I won't," he quickly assured her, relieved to have successfully negotiated the emotional minefield.

But Piper wasn't finished, so he wasn't quite out of it yet. "I'm going to be giving you my opinion about potential work partners. I don't expect you to agree with everything I say, but I do expect you to truly consider it. If you're not going to take me seriously, then let's stop wasting time."

"I do take you seriously." More than she knew.

A piece of hair blew across her face and their hands collided as both reached to brush it away. She gave him a stern look and started walking again. "No flirting and no trying to dazzle women with your charm."

He grinned. "You're taking all the fun out of it."

"Mark—"

"Relax. I'll dial it down."

They took several more steps before she said, "You don't need to work that hard, you know. You're so dynamically good-looking that when you pour it on, women are overwhelmed."

"I'm...not sure how to respond to that. Thank you?"

She smiled briefly. "I'm not telling you anything you don't already know."

He hadn't known she found him "dynamically good-looking."

"Just be extra-aware of your effect on women you're interviewing," she cautioned.

"You're not going to recommend anyone who'll be overwhelmed by my godlike handsomeness."

She laughed and flashed him a brilliant smile. "You're right! Very good."

For just a second, he'd glimpsed the woman behind the professional mask, the way she'd respond and look at him if she weren't maintaining a professional distance. He wanted to see more of that woman. Mark's breath caught as something reached inside him, grabbed hold of his heart and squeezed. *She could be the one.* No. His hand fisted against his thigh. He'd really gone soft if a laugh and a smile had him thinking mushy thoughts. He didn't do mushy.

He didn't do relationships, period.

Clearing his throat, he asked, "So, uh, what's next? How does this work?"

WELL, THAT HADN'T WORKED.

Piper had hoped that by addressing his attraction to women with him matter-of-factly, it would neutralize its effect on her and turn it into a doctor-patient thing.

Nope.

As they walked on a sidewalk made uneven by tree roots, he occasionally stepped close enough to brush her arm or for her to feel a minute warming in the air temperature because of his body heat. Even within the thick hoodie she wore, the hairs on her arms raised when he was close enough to touch.

Anger hadn't worked, either, especially when it meant she wanted to beat her fists against his chest and then fling herself against it as his arms encircled her right before he kissed her passionately.

In the middle of the sidewalk.

No, scratch anger.

Remaining detached wasn't working, either, especially when he stared into her eyes and made her feel all twitchy inside.

She was just so *aware* of him and he wasn't even trying. And when he did try, he didn't mean it. Yet, she still reacted and it baffled her.

When he'd reached to brush the stupid wig hair off her face, she'd banged his hand out of the way, because all she needed was to feel his fingers against her cheek and her face would get that zombie-sex-slave look on it.

I just can't help myself, she'd heard clients—and her mother—tell her over and over. She'd thought they were weak and self-indulgent. Now, not so much. Fighting an unwanted attraction was exhausting.

Fortunately, Mark had just asked her how she planned to proceed. Piper might as well begin right now because the sooner she found someone to work with him, the less chance she had of embarrassing herself. Again.

"I have a general compatibility survey I'll have you fill out. Based on what I learn from that, I'll ask you questions," she told him.

"What kind of questions?"

"Let's see… In your case, I'll want to know your relationship style." She had a pretty good idea already. Cut to the chase. And there was never much of a chase. "You don't formally date because of your lifestyle."

"Right."

"And I noticed everything you demonstrated to Medina was quick and to the point, with no time wasted on the preliminaries. No subtlety."

"Hey." He glanced down at her.

"Not a criticism. You live at a faster pace. I'm guessing you can't spend a lot of time forming relationships."

He shook his head.

"As an adult, how long was your longest relationship? It doesn't have to be romantic." Although she was unprofessionally curious.

"How are you defining relationship?"

Typical wary male. "One where you interacted on a frequent and regular basis that resulted in you and the other party considering each other's feelings and learning intimate details of each other's lives."

"How intimate?" he asked cautiously.

Do. Not. Blush. "What you'd learn from living with someone or from a longtime friend. I'm not talking one-night stands, here."

Mark nodded, but she could tell he didn't want to answer. Probably didn't want to think about it, either.

"I haven't really had a long-term relationship."

Piper wasn't surprised. "Roommates?"

"Not since freshman year in the dorm."

"Okay, that counts. So nine or ten months."

"No." He grimaced. "He wasn't someone I'd consider a friend. I certainly didn't care what he did and his intimate habits were disgusting."

Piper gave a short laugh. "I get the picture."

"And I'm sorry for that."

"How about your longest work relationship?"

"Working for OMG, I guess. Four years."

"Hmm. That's not exactly your typical eight-to-five job. I was looking for one where you show up regularly and see the same people and interact with them."

Mark hunched his shoulders. "Some part-time jobs, I guess."

When Mark said he worked alone, he meant alone. She foresaw a bumpy road ahead.

"I'm guessing you were an only child."

"Yes."

"What about friends?"

"I've got plenty of friends." He scowled as he spoke. "I meet people all over the world."

Since she'd started asking questions, he'd looked into the store windows they passed, watched the birds pick at crumbs on the sidewalk and gazed into the trees every time the leaves rustled in the breeze. Anywhere but at her.

Piper backed off on the questions until they reached the end of the block, waited for the light to change and crossed the street. Then she asked, "Who's your closest friend?"

Mark exhaled heavily and appeared to study the menu on a cafe's chalk sign as they walked past. "Travis, I guess."

That would be news to Travis. "Does Travis think of you as his friend?" she asked carefully.

"He got me out of a Mexican mountain camp," Mark said harshly. "I'd call that being a friend."

"So you guys hang out and drink beer, watch sports together, that kind of thing?" she pressed.

Mark gritted his teeth. "It's not that kind of friendship. I've got plenty of journalist buddies for that."

"Who would you ask to dogsit?"

"I don't have a dog."

"Of course not. Uh…who do you ask to water your plants, collect your mail and keep an eye on your place when you're gone?"

"No plants, I have a post office box and great building security."

Piper tamped down her irritation. If he wouldn't make this easy for her, she wouldn't make it easy for him. "Who inherits your stuff?"

He looked down at her in disbelief. "My mom. But what's it matter? When it comes to that, I won't care."

"I'm trying to find a relationship you've had so I can learn things like how you resolve conflicts, what sets you off, whether you've got a short fuse or a long fuse, whether you're a morning person or a night owl, how you decompress—"

"I get that," he interrupted her. "But walking along the streets of Austin while I spill my guts isn't my idea of a good time."

Piper guessed he wouldn't like spilling his guts under any circumstances. "It's different when you're the one being interviewed."

"It is," he admitted. "I'd much rather ask the questions."

"Then ask me one."

She'd surprised him.

"Okay. What's your longest relationship?"

And now he'd surprised her. "Dancie," she answered promptly. "We've been friends since sophomore year of college. She let me live with her rent free for a couple of years or I would have had to quit school. She got me the gig with OMG, too. I owe her."

"She sounds like a good friend."

There was wistfulness in his voice and Piper knew he'd be appalled that she'd heard it.

"She is. It's interesting. I've got one really close friend and you have lots of casual friends."

"What can I say?" He smiled without humor. "Different lifestyles."

The truth was that Mark had a lot of acquaintances, but nobody actually knew him. They knew *about* him. He presented the world with a good-looking, confident exterior and a glamorous, exciting job. Hundreds of thousands read all about his adventures and he was the envy of the entire *Guys of Texas* readership.

Piper would bet that she knew the man behind the image better than anyone else. And about that image… "How much of that stuff you wrote for Travis is true?"

He grinned. "You read my columns?"

"Some," she admitted. "You were the competition. So?"

"It's all true," he told her. "But they're more about the sizzle than the meat."

"Even the ones about being captured?"

His jaw hardened. "Not those. It's not a thing to glamorize. Besides, there are people who helped me who could suffer for it."

"How long were you held hostage?"

"Five months." Absently, he rubbed his wrist. "Could we please not discuss it?"

In Piper's experience, when a client didn't want to discuss something, that was exactly what they should be discussing. But he'd said *please*. He hadn't flat-out refused. And for a man like Mark, that was a huge concession.

So Piper said, "Okay." Ironically, the relationship with his captors was the longest he'd told her about so far.

Nodding, he dropped his arm.

"Mark?"

"Hmm?"

"Could I see your wrist?"

"There's nothing to see."

Piper stopped walking.

Mark continued for half a dozen steps before he stopped. She watched his shoulders rise and fall.

"Fine." he said. As he walked back to her, he unbuttoned his cuff and peeled it back. "Here." He thrust his arm out.

Although she'd half expected to see the faded pink scar line from where his wrist had been bound, the sight made the breath hiss between her teeth. She knew he'd been a hostage, and knew his leg had been hurt. But seeing the scar from where he'd been tied up for who knows how long made her want to wrap her arms around him and never let go.

"Oh, Mark." Gently, she ran her fingertips over the bumpy ridge. It was wider in some places than others. Different bindings? Hours of struggling to escape?

She looked up to find his head close, his eyes searching hers. "They must have kept you tied up for days!"

He barely nodded.

"Is your other wrist this bad?"

He slowly moved his head from side to side. "This one got infected."

"I'm so sorry."

"Not your fault."

"But still."

A man who endured this, a man who survived this, was not a man who would waste time worrying about whose turn it was to make travel arrangements or wondering if his partner's feelings were hurt because he'd spoken abruptly. Conflict resolution style? Deal with it and move on.

When he was given an opportunity, he took it. He didn't lose it by thinking about all the things that could go wrong. He acted. If he made a mistake, he dealt with it and didn't look back.

Piper should be more like that. She was doing nothing while she waited for the perfect man and the perfect moment.

Mark couldn't stand doing nothing and had the scars on his wrists to prove it. He'd had no way of knowing when, or if, he'd ever be freed. As the months passed, he must have thought he'd been forgotten.

Surprising herself, Piper bent and softly kissed his wrist before smoothing his cuff back into place. When she finished fastening the button, she looked up, but he didn't speak or move away. Neither did she.

The breeze blew hair into her face again, but this time, when Mark raised his hand to brush the strands away, she let him.

His fingers moved against her cheek making her yearn for more of his touch. And if she didn't step back and stop gazing into his eyes, he'd know it.

Mark slowly looped the hair behind her ear. He left his hand resting against the side of her neck, his thumb brushing the sensitive area beneath her earlobe.

He was going to kiss her unless she moved away. And he

was making sure she knew it. No dazzling smile—with or without dimples—no cheesy lines, no suggestive body language. Just Mark. And that was plenty.

Here was opportunity waiting for her. Was she going to grab it or let it go?

His thumb brushed against her earlobe, sending shivers racing over Piper's body. She tilted her chin up. Mark lowered his head and his lips gently met hers.

For a few seconds, that's all it was—two pairs of lips saying "hello." Then Mark moved his hand to the back of her neck and drew her close and it became, "Well, hellloooo."

Mark brushed his lips against hers in a tender exploration that completely undid her. She'd expected a practiced kiss, meant to quickly excite her. Quick and to the point—wasn't that how he normally operated? No subtlety?

But Mark was taking it surprisingly slow, his lips barely parted, seemingly just fine with soft movements that tickled awake all her senses. His lips were warm and soft without being mushy. He smelled faintly of Friezen Burger, but then she did, too. And beneath that, his scent was appealingly male, all warm and rich. No sharp tang or mustiness. She opened her mouth a little wider and pressed closer, tasting him.

"Piper," he breathed and she inhaled his breath. She wanted more.

How long had she waited to find a man who made her want more? Since her college boyfriend. She remembered the hours and hours they'd kissed and touched and stared into each other's eyes until she wanted to climb into his skin with him.

And she remembered how she'd known when she'd lost him. He'd smelled and tasted different. No longer warm and rich, but cool and metallic. Wrong.

Mark cradled her head and deepened the kiss just the slightest bit. When his fingers stroked her nape, Piper wound her arms around him and tried to avoid melting into a little puddle.

She was barely aware of voices approaching before Mark shifted them away from the sidewalk, twisting so her back was against the live oak, all without breaking their kiss.

Piper smiled against his mouth because it was such a smooth Mark Banning move. She tightened her arms and he settled against her, pressing their bodies together.

He was warm and solid and he wanted her. Piper felt a rush of feeling and opened her mouth, inviting him inside. When his tongue gently stroked hers, a tiny sound escaped. Closer. She wanted him closer. She rolled her hips forward and brought her hands underneath his jacket to stroke his back.

This slow, deliberate build wasn't at all the way she thought he'd kiss. She'd expected him to take the lead and, well, attempt to seduce her with dazzling technique because that was the Mark Banning way. But he'd kept his hands cradling her face and occasionally stroking the side of her neck, while he simply kissed her, only deepening the kiss when she initiated it.

He'd be shocked if she told him these simple, slow, deliberate kisses were much more effective because they were much more intimate. But Mark Banning avoided intimacy and embraced the shallow. Piper felt sorry for him because he would never experience a connection with another person like this. It was strange how she thought of Mark Banning as a completely separate person from the Mark she knew. From the Mark she was currently kissing.

She was kissing the real Mark. The realization shook her. He was opening himself up to her, letting her connect emotionally. Bonding with her. Making her care.

How could he do this to her? He *knew,* he had to know connecting emotionally would make her fall for him. Why would he do it? To prove he could? Didn't he care that she'd be hurt when he left? And he would leave. He worked alone. She got that. He'd told her often enough.

Yeah, he was a loner, wild and untamed. Undomesticated and destined to remain so. The stuff of legends. Daring and brave, with dashing good looks. A romantic fantasy come to life. And so on and so forth.

He was good for heart-pounding thrills and exciting memories, not for everyday life.

She'd forgotten how powerful good chemistry could be and had become impatient with women who made poor choices because of it.

Like her mother.

Piper yanked her hands from beneath his jacket and pulled her mouth away abruptly.

What was she doing? Standing against a tree next to a public sidewalk in front of business establishments and sending "kiss me" signals to a client, that's what. And Mark had very politely obliged. Sure, the kiss had lingered, but who's to say he couldn't enjoy being polite? Especially when she'd been so very enthusiastic.

Even now, as he stepped back and let his arms fall away, he was polite and restrained, all the things she hadn't been. How could she have forgotten where she was? And who she was with?

Cringing, she remembered lecturing him about flirting and manipulating women. And he hadn't. No, this was all Piper's doing. Every step, every wiggle, every moan. How mortifying.

He gazed at her questioningly and she noted that he hadn't protested or suggested they continue elsewhere. Not that she would have.

Or, at least she hoped her sense of propriety would have kicked in. No guarantees, though.

"That was…" she began.

"Great?"

Well, yes. "Unprofessional."

"Are you saying I kiss like an amateur?"

"No!" She darted a glance at his amused face. She was so glad he was enjoying himself at her expense. The mighty had fallen and all that. "I meant—"

"I know what you meant," he interrupted, saving her the embarrassment of saying the words. "But we're not in your office and you're still undercover." He tugged gently on her wig. "Call it staying in character."

Mark was offering her a face-saving out and Piper was almost desperate enough to take it: "That's no excuse."

"Cut yourself some slack." He dropped a hand on her shoulder and squeezed briefly as though she were a team member who'd made a bad play. "You were trying to get to know me and you can learn a lot from a kiss."

That's what she was afraid of. "True, and you know what? I've learned enough that it's not necessary for you to walk all the way to my office. Besides, your car is back there." She gestured vaguely.

"I don't mind the exercise," he said.

"Yes, but the questionnaire I told you about is way too basic. We've covered most of the information already, so we can skip that." She couldn't look at him. "I have a pretty good idea of the type of woman you need."

"But what about the woman I want?" he asked lightly.

"Uh…" She nervously tucked her hair behind her ear. "It's up to you and Travis to send me qualified applicants. I'll screen them and send my recommendations on to you. You interview them and if you find someone, great. If not, we'll keep looking."

She felt him staring down at her. "Do I need to schedule any follow-up appointments with you?" he asked.

Piper forced herself to meet his eyes. "No. We're done."

9

Step nine: If you haven't already, introduce him to your friends and listen to their opinion. If they don't like him, why do you?

"TRAVIS SENT THESE OVER." Dancie dropped a stack of résumés on Piper's desk.

"Thanks."

Instead of leaving, Dancie planted her hands on either side of the résumés, her newly straightened hair swinging forward. Piper didn't know if she would ever get used to a Dancie with straight hair.

"Did you make a deal with Travis?"

Piper had wanted to wait until she found Mark a partner before saying anything to Dancie. She should have known Travis wouldn't keep his mouth shut. "Yes. He agreed to let you use your old office if I find Mark a partner both he and your dad will accept."

Stone-faced, Dancie slowly straightened. "Without discussing it with me first?"

"There wasn't time. The opportunity came up and I grabbed it." Isn't that what Dancie was always telling her to do?

"Why?"

"Because it's too crowded with you here." Piper gestured to the doorway. "There's no soundproofing in the wall. It's like you and Anna are in the room with me. You hear my clients and we can hear you." Remembering how Dancie had let Piper live with her made the next part difficult to say. "It's just not working."

"Why didn't you say something before you went whining to Travis?"

She's angry because you went to Travis, not because you found her someplace else to work. "I didn't go to Travis and I certainly didn't whine. And, Dancie, I did ask you to keep it down. More than once."

"And we did!"

For about two seconds, Piper thought. "I was sitting in Friezen's when Travis called me about helping Mark, which I was reluctant to do."

Dancie tilted her head, studying her. Uh-oh. "You told me he's the most arrogant, egotistical jerk you'd ever met and you never wanted to see him again. Is that what you consider reluctant?"

Now was not the time to go into Mark's hidden qualities. "I know you don't want to spend money on office space yet, so when I realized Travis was desperate, I took advantage of the situation."

Dancie slowly shook her head.

"It's just the use of the office," Piper told her. "I stressed that you weren't going back to work for OMG."

"I'm not mooching free office space from them, either. He and Dad would always claim they'd helped me get started. And they'd be right. I want to show them we can do this on our own."

So using her mom's cash was different, Piper supposed. Was she going to argue about that? Not a chance.

"The Piper Plan is going to be huge," Dancie said. "Surely it's worth a couple of weeks of inconvenience."

More like a couple of months, Piper bet. "It's not the inconvenience. I owe my clients confidentiality and privacy. You can hear everything and, incidentally, so can they. I'm not thrilled that they're privy to details about my new business venture."

"What about Anna? She's been able to hear everything, too."

"But until you moved in here, I had no idea how much. So points to Anna for discretion."

"Thank you!" they heard.

They caught each other's eyes and broke into laughter, the tension evaporating.

"Point taken," Dancie said. "But I don't want to blow my start-up capital on office rental, so how about this. I'll try to be away when you have clients coming in. I can work at home or, better yet, I'll bring my laptop to Mikey's and work on the web interface there."

Piper raised her eyebrows. "Mikey?"

"Our web guy." Dancie tucked her hair behind her ear and avoided Piper's eyes.

She likes him. Piper smothered her smile. Finally, a man had caught Dancie's interest. She'd been even worse than Piper about finding a man she liked.

"If you were gone, that would really help. And maybe Anna can group my in-person appointments so we can have blocks of time when you know you can work here. It'll be more efficient for me, anyway."

"I'm on it," they heard.

"Thanks, Anna." Piper didn't have to raise her voice.

"That works for me," Dancie agreed. She picked up the stack she'd brought in. "I'll take these back to Travis."

"Why?"

Dancie looked puzzled. "I know how much Mark pissed

you off. And showing up at Friezen's like that..." Dancie shook her head. "You've been twitchy ever since you got back yesterday."

Piper shifted in her office chair. Twitchy was one way to describe it.

"The fact that you were still willing to work with him to help me is why I'm not more angry at you right now. But we've arranged the working situation here, so you don't have to take him as a client now." She turned to leave.

"Uh...hang on."

Slowly, Dancie did an about-face and eyed her warily.

Yeah, it was hard to hide stuff from someone who knew you well, but that didn't stop Piper from trying. "I gave my word."

"So ungive it."

"He already made an appointment. It'll be okay."

Dancie walked very slowly to the desk and set the stack of résumés on it. Then she looked at Piper. "Be careful."

MARK WAS NOT THE TYPE who looked back. The past was the past and he couldn't change it. The future held no guarantees, so he concentrated on living in the present. He did allow himself to feel regret on occasion. He even, in spite of what Piper thought—and apparently most of the media world as well—considered several possible courses of action before taking one. He simply considered quickly and operated on his first impression or gut feeling most of the time. He'd found that dwelling on the problem or overthinking it either made it bigger or led him right back to his original impulse, anyway.

So thinking about Piper and considering calling her when he actually dreamed about her—*dreamed,* for God's sake— was not beneficial. His first opinion, that getting involved with her wouldn't work and would probably result in a hugely messy complication, was the right one. No, it was the *correct* one. That didn't make it right.

Mark set down the new electronic tablet he was testing for this next assignment. Right. Testing it by cyber-stalking Piper. He drew a breath and blew it out in disgust. He told himself he was "checking her credentials." Except for the fact that it should have been something he'd done *before* approaching her, it was a plausible lie. Too bad he didn't believe it. It was a sorry day when a man couldn't lie to himself.

Walking over to the tiny balcony of his condo, Mark slid open the glass, and stepped outside. The night air was cool, but lacked the crispness he'd sought to clear his head. He stared at the Austin skyline and the brightly lit streets below. Faintly, he could hear laughter and the heavy bass of music being played outdoors as university students partied.

The truth, unpalatable though it was, was that he wanted to see Piper again. Not to work, just to be with her. He didn't like the questions she asked, or more accurately, didn't like his answers. She stirred up bad memories and invaded his dreams. And still he wanted to be with her.

It was that damn kiss. It had been sweet. *Sweet.* Not a word anyone used to describe him or anything about him. Mark Banning didn't do sweet. So what had that been about? He'd barely touched her and she'd melted in his arms. He'd been content to keep kissing her and kissing her, even when he'd pressed her against the tree and his body wanted more.

When he'd kissed her, he'd felt…things. He didn't want to name those things, either. Didn't want to think about them. But that one kiss had affected him more profoundly than any he'd given or received during the most passionate lovemaking. It had affected her, too, judging by her shocked expression. She hadn't welcomed the feelings it aroused any more than he had, as demonstrated by her refusal to see him again. Not that he'd asked to see her again, but the implication was there.

We're done.

Hell of an implication.

Gripping the railing, Mark inhaled deeply. She might be able to ignore that kind of a kiss, but he couldn't. Wouldn't.

No, they weren't done. They were just getting started.

"ARE THOSE THE LUCKY winners?" Dancie came to stand next to her by the file table in Piper's office.

Piper nodded. On the long table, she'd grouped the résumés with photographs clipped to them. As Dancie watched, Piper moved one between groups, made a frustrated sound, and moved it back.

"Piper, their rank doesn't matter if they're all going to interview with Mark."

"It does matter. This is like a chess game. I'm sending him these applicants first." She pointed to the group on the far left. "And he's going to reject them all."

"Then don't send them to him."

"I have to," Piper said. "He's going to reject the first group no matter what because he wants to establish that he's important and unique and complex, and that it won't be easy to find someone worthy. He wants me to work at it."

"You have been working at it," Dancie argued. "Some might say obsessively, but I'm not going to."

"He has to see the effort I've made. Trust me on this," Piper told her. "So, I'm saving the best candidates for the second round. But if I don't give him some pretty good ones in the first batch, he'll figure out what I'm doing and reject those *and* the second group." She tapped the résumé she'd moved. "But I hate to sacrifice this one because she's really good."

"Maybe he won't reject her."

"Oh, he will," Piper said. "She spells Jinger with a *J*."

"Huh?"

Piper waved her hand. "Never mind."

"What if he surprises you and picks one in the first group just to get it over with?"

"Then he'll miss the best candidates!" She gazed at Dancie

in indecision. "And if she doesn't work out, he'll say 'See? You don't know what you're talking about.'"

Dancie bent down and moved Jinger to the first group, picked them up and handed them to Piper. "You're overthinking again. Let him interview these."

As Piper predicted, after a morning of interviews, Mark summarily rejected the entire first group.

"You called that right." Dancie handed her half a roasted-veggie sub and set a medium iced tea on the filing table.

It was a couple of days later and there had been complete silence from Mark. According to the candidates, he'd told them all the same thing—that he was going to keep looking and he didn't want to leave them in limbo when they could be interviewing for another position. He'd even pointed out weak areas in their work experience or suggested job leads. One gushingly reported that he'd helped her with her interviewing skills.

Saint Mark.

Although he did tell Jinger that constantly having to spell her name to interviewers would be a distraction and slow her down. Fair enough.

Piper and Dancie studied the second group of candidates as they ate their lunch. "Are you going to send him all seven of these?" Dancie asked her.

Piper chewed on the end of her iced tea straw. "I haven't decided yet. Either of these two—" and she separated them from the rest of the applicants "—would be perfect. This one is in her mid-forties and has worked overseas. She took time off when her kids were younger and now wants back in. She's got three teenagers—she'll be able to deal with Mark. The other one is mid-thirties, but still a little older than Mark and wants to break out of a small domestic market. She's got six brothers and sisters, so I know she'll be able to handle Mark, as well."

"So what's the problem?" Dancie asked.

"Do I send them with the rest? Or do I split the group in case he's not through making his point to OMG?"

"What did he say was wrong with the first batch?" Dancie bit into her sandwich.

"He didn't." Piper took off the top of her bun. She'd eaten too much bread lately.

"You mean he refused to tell you?"

Piper took a bite of sandwich.

Dancie, recognizing the evading tactic for what it was, waited until Piper swallowed. "You did ask, didn't you?"

"I heard from the women he interviewed. I haven't talked to him, directly." Piper opened her mouth but Dancie held her wrist to keep her from taking another bite.

"Why not?"

"I figured he'd call me if he had anything to say."

"You're avoiding him." Dancie released Piper's wrist. "And you're still twitchy. Now I'm really worried."

"Don't be."

"You do know you have to talk to him before you send him the next batch."

"Not necessarily." Piper stared unseeingly at her sandwich.

"Yes, you do!" Dancie insisted. "Find out why he didn't like anyone and then you'll know whether you need to split that last group or not."

"Okay. I'll email him." Piper took another bite of her sandwich.

"Chicken. And I don't mean the sandwich." Dancie set hers on the wrapper and brushed her hands together. Then she rolled her chair back until she could reach Piper's desk phone. Turning it around, she held out the receiver. "Swallow and call him. You need to be able to hear his voice when you discuss this. Guys don't communicate well in email."

"I'm still eating," Piper protested. "I'll call him after we go over the website."

Dancie looked down at the discarded bread and the rest of the sandwich Piper held. "Are you going to eat that bread?"

"No."

"Then you're a bite away from done. No sense putting it off. Take this."

Piper popped the last bite into her mouth and took the receiver.

"Call," Dancie ordered.

Piper pointed to her mouth.

"You can dial and chew at the same time."

When had Dancie become so bossy? Fine. She'd call him. Piper waved her away. Dancie shook her head, not budging. Mark was probably at lunch, anyway. Piper punched in his office number and swallowed.

No answer. Breathing easier, she hung up without leaving a message. "I'll try again later." Maybe.

"Coward," Dancie said.

"Because I didn't leave a message? He'll see my number on caller ID. He'll know why I called and if he feels like calling me back, he will."

But Dancie wouldn't quit. "Have you got his cell number?"

Piper pointed to a sticky note that Dancie had to read upside down.

Trying to keep her breath even, Piper tapped in the number. "See? I'm calling. You don't have to wait," she told Dancie while the phone rang.

"Ha" was Dancie's comment.

When the call rolled over into Mark's voice mail, Piper was relieved. She did not want to have a conversation with Mark in front of Dancie. She could cite confidentiality, but Dancie wouldn't buy it.

Piper hadn't spoken to Mark since the other day. *Twitchy* didn't begin to describe her conflicted emotions. She was drawn to Mark, who'd turned out to be both more and less than typical of his type.

She didn't trust herself to keep her voice neutral if Dancie listened in. Especially if Mark brought up the kiss. But why would he? She'd totally exaggerated it in her mind. It was a brief moment. She'd felt sympathetic. He'd gone through a horrible ordeal. It was only one, sweet little kiss.

One that snuck past her defenses and turned into a bigger kiss.

A sneaky kiss.

So, she gave the receiver back to Dancie and shrugged. "No answer. He's probably in class. I'll just email."

Dancie gave her a look and withdrew her cell phone. She pressed a number. "Hey, Travis—where's Mark? He's not answering his cell, but we want to set up interviews with this next batch of candidates. Okay, thanks. I'll tell her."

Dancie ended the call, set her phone down and picked up her sandwich. "He's at PT."

Piper gathered up her lunch trash. "I'll catch up with him later."

Dancie sipped her tea and said nothing.

"I will."

Piper balled everything up and tossed it toward the wastebasket two feet away. She missed. Conscious of Dancie watching, Piper picked up the ball and a stray napkin and dropped them into the trash. The napkin fluttered just outside the basket. Seriously? Exhaling, Piper stooped to retrieve it and placed it carefully into the wastebasket.

"Hmm," Dancie commented.

"Dancie, calling Mark is no big deal. Really."

"Then why are you twitching?"

"Why do you keep using that word?"

"Because it fits." Dancie examined her sandwich and pulled out a strand of shredded lettuce. Dangling it over her open mouth, she dropped it in.

"Whenever you're finished playing with your food, we can

go over the mock-up for the Piper Plan website." If Piper didn't know better, she'd think Dancie was waiting for something.

And then Piper's desk phone rang. Dancie met her eyes. Bingo.

"Piper Scott," she answered.

"Hey, it's Mark. Travis said you were trying to get ahold of me."

"That was thoughtful of Travis." She spoke in a sugar-sweet voice and directed a venomous gaze toward Dancie, who was avidly watching her. "Mark, I'm putting you on speaker. Dancie is with me." Which ought to nix any personal talk.

"Sure. But I've only got a couple of minutes now. I'm about to get hooked up to a heat-therapy machine and won't be able to take my phone in with me. You could actually come and talk with me here. You'd be doing me a favor, because I'm at the mercy of whatever they've got on the TV for the next hour. You might get kind of sweaty, though."

An image of a sweaty Mark Banning popped into her mind. A shirtless—and she had to use her imagination—Mark, muscles glistening, unable to walk away, completely at her mercy, clouds of heavy steam surrounding them, shielding them from other eyes as she ran her hands over his slick—

"Piper?"

"Uh...that's okay. I just wondered if you had any overall comments or concerns before I send the next group."

"I've been thinking about that. Since I can't have an intern to boss around, I'm looking for someone with more experience. I'm not going to do any on-the-job training. She's got to be able to function independently."

"It's up to you and Travis to vet the credentials. I can only work from the names you give me. However, I will remind you that the more experience someone has, the less you'll be able to 'boss her around' and the more she'll want to contribute to your story."

"I don't share bylines," he said, flatly. "At the most, she gets a producer credit. Make sure anyone I interview will be okay with that."

"Got it. Let me tweak the parameters of my search criteria and send you my recommendations."

Dancie caught her attention. *Tweak the parameters of your search criteria?* she mouthed and rolled her eyes.

Piper gave her a warning look.

"Thanks, but I don't need to see them first," Mark said. "Do me a favor and set up the interviews for tomorrow morning. If anyone can't make it then, I could see them after six, but I'd prefer not to."

Piper opened her mouth to tell him that was *not* her job, when Dancie cut in. "Sure, Mark. Did you want Piper to be there, too?"

Shaking her head, Piper vehemently crossed her hands over each other. "Dancie, we've already discussed that. It's better if Mark interviews one-on-one."

There was a short, charged silence before Mark said, "If you change your mind, I don't have a problem with you being there, too. So if we're all set, they're ready for me here."

"Okay. Dancie—" and she emphasized the name ever so slightly "—will let you know the interview schedule."

"You practically hung up on him," Dancie said after the call ended.

Piper turned to her. "What are you doing? No. I get what you're doing. Why are you doing it?"

"You like him."

"Leave it alone, Dancie."

"Why? He likes you, too."

"Because he 'doesn't have a problem with me being there'? That's a big stretch."

"No, because he's going to pass on the next group, too, and then he'll invite you somewhere to discuss it. Only he's really going to use the opportunity to make his move."

Thud. Thud. Thud. *Oh, stop it,* Piper told herself. "Well, I'm not giving him that opportunity."

"You're looking at this thing with Mark in entirely the wrong way," Dancie told her. "This is a unique opportunity."

"There is no 'thing' with Mark," Piper insisted, to herself as well as Dancie. "There isn't going to be a 'thing' with Mark. He's leaving after the first of the year. It would be stupid to have a 'thing' with Mark."

"Really? You've followed your own plan, but when you meet your perfect man, you don't like him. No sparks. No love connection."

How had Dancie known?

"So either The Piper Plan is flawed and we'd better fix it before it goes live, or you lied on your own compatibility questionnaire."

"Why would I do that?"

"I don't know. Why would you?"

Piper narrowed her eyes. "I didn't."

"Maybe not intentionally. But you've got the hots for Mark Banning and you need to find out what it is that he's got that you want."

"Oh, I know what he's got that I want," Piper mumbled.

"*That's* what I'm talking about." Dancie jabbed her finger. "I'll bet you rated a hot body low on your list of desirable traits because you think it sounds shallow."

"It is shallow."

"So what? It's one thing, not everything. You're not your mother."

Piper was getting angry. "I know I'm not. I also know that you're taking up all the time I'd blocked to review the website this afternoon. So save the lecture for another time and let's get to work."

The outer door opened and closed. "Hey, Anna," Dancie called.

Anna appeared in the doorway. "What's up?"

"Would you make a run to the Croissant Cafe for a couple of chocolate croissants with mocha cream?"

"Sure."

"And get one for yourself. There's money in my purse. Take your time."

Anna looked from one to the other. "Gotcha."

Piper could get up and walk out with Anna. How many of her clients had become defensive and had done just that when she told them truths they didn't want to hear?

But she was going to sit here and listen to what Dancie, her closest friend, had to say.

Dancie waited until Anna left. "You've spent your life trying not to be your mother. Okay. Mission accomplished. What's next?"

"I don't know. I guess I'll have to figure that out."

"Mark can help you."

"No!" Piper's voice sounded loud and tinged with panic. If she could recognize it, so could Dancie.

"Why not?"

"Because he's not the right kind of man for me."

"I know, he's leaving. That's why he's ideal. You already know he's not rejecting you—he's leaving because of his job. You won't be invested in the relationship, and if getting involved turns out to be a mistake, he'll be gone soon, anyway."

"It's stupid to go into something knowing you'll be hurt. Isn't that what I tell all those women who keep falling for bad boys? And then when he acts like a bad boy and they get hurt, they want me to tell them how to get him to stop being a bad boy. But if he did, they wouldn't like him anymore."

Dancie looked intrigued. "Is Mark a bad boy?"

"No." Piper hesitated. "Maybe a little. The point is that I don't want to get hurt."

"Piper! Oh, my God, if you already know you could fall for the guy so hard it'll hurt when he leaves in a couple of months, then you absolutely have to find out why."

She made sense, but Piper wasn't sure if it was because Dancie actually was right or because Piper wanted her to be right. "Then what?"

"When it's over, you fill out the Piper Plan questionnaire again. And promise me you'll answer with what you want, not what you think you should want."

Piper sighed. "How about I skip getting my heart broken and just fill out the questionnaire now?"

"Listen to you! Did you ever think it might work out between the two of you?"

Piper shook her head. "That would be just stupid. Really, really stupid."

"But if he tries to set something up, and I think he will, you have to go."

And then Dancie did something horrible and awful. "Even though you've paid me back, I know you've always felt you owed me because I helped you."

"Oh, no."

Dancie nodded. "I'm asking you to accept if Mark wants to see you. You don't even have to make the first move."

"What if he doesn't?"

She smiled. "I may not be the expert on men in this room, but I bet a chocolate croissant he will."

10

Step ten: Beware of the pseudotype. Has he been concealing traits that caused you to mistype him? He may not be your perfect man after all.

"A MOTORCYCLE? YOU didn't say anything about a motorcycle." Piper stared at the big, black hulking thing parked on the street in front of her apartment. Because, yes, everything had played out just as Dancie had predicted. Mark hadn't liked any of the women he'd interviewed and wanted to meet with her to discuss it. And Piper had agreed because Dancie had turned out to be a ruthless negotiator.

But Dancie had not predicted a motorcycle. She couldn't hold Piper to her promise to see Mark when it involved riding a motorcycle, could she?

He'd told her he wanted her to meet some friends and Piper had been surprised and touched, not to mention really curious. But now that she knew motorcycles were involved, not so much.

Mark stood beside her, grinning happily. "I didn't know if my leg had healed enough for me to ride yet. And then my bike had been in storage for so long, I spent most of yesterday working on it so it would pass inspection. I pulled in right as the place closed, but I told the guy I'd been waiting to ride my bike for over a year and wasn't sure I could hold off until Monday. Bottom line, it passed, and I can take you riding today." He looked down at her and his whole face was pure, uncomplicated joy.

Piper's was pure, uncomplicated terror.

"Anyway, in case it didn't work out, I didn't want you to be disappointed."

"How…thoughtful." She gave him a determined smile because he looked so happy and she'd never seen him looking so happy.

Piper could tell from his gush of words that he'd been afraid his injury wouldn't allow him to ride again. He was elated. Elated looked good on him, as did the leather riding jacket.

"Come on. I brought a jacket, gloves and helmet for you." The way he grabbed her hand and drew her toward the bike made him seem younger. It was as though he'd shed his skin. The Mark Banning skin.

It was a compliment. He felt he could drop the facade with her. That's exactly what she wanted; to get to know the real Mark Banning. He apparently loved motorcycles.

Okay. Okay, she could do this. She was not going to spoil it for him.

"Isn't this the most perfect Sunday afternoon ever? Last night's cool front blew all the pollen out of the air." He paused to take a deep breath and look around him before he unbuckled the saddle pouch and removed the jacket for her.

It looked exactly like his, and both were mercifully free of tacky logos.

He held it out for her and she slipped her arms into it, immediately catching a faint whiff of another woman's perfume.

She wasn't going to ask. Her fingers fumbled with the zipper and she felt him watching her.

"Here, let me help you with that." He hooked the edges together and zipped her up like a little kid.

Clearly, he could hardly wait to get back on his bike. Piper would have smiled if her lips hadn't been numb with fear.

"And the helmet." He handed it to her.

She turned it over in her hands and tried to figure out how it worked. It shouldn't be *that* hard.

"Piper Scott, you've never ridden before."

She gave a quick shake of her head.

"You are in for a treat." He took the helmet from her and positioned it to go on her head. "It's like you're flying. After a while, you're part of the machine and you don't even think about steering. You just do."

Piper held her head up, bracing for the helmet. "My mother would just love you."

He grinned and lifted the helmet. "No one has ever said that to me." Then he noticed her expression and lowered his arms. "Why do I get the feeling it isn't a compliment?"

She stared at the bike, remembering. "My mom loved motorcycle guys. And men with pickups, too. I spent my childhood watching them drive into and out of our lives. Unfortunately, they always left with a lovely parting gift from Mom. Usually cash. Usually cash we needed for something else. And then when mom realized they weren't coming back and neither was her money, we'd move so she could 'get a fresh start.' The fresh starts usually happened at night and we could only take what we could cram into the car."

Mark was silent for several beats. "I'm torn between stating the obvious—that I'm not one of your mom's boyfriends—and asking what kind of bikes they drove. I think I'll settle for saying I'm sorry you went through that."

He made her smile. "Big and noisy," she told him.

"The bikes?" He laughed and hoisted the helmet once more.

He showed her how to kind of roll it onto her head. She

waited while he made a few adjustments to the fit, and fastened the chin strap for her.

"Feel okay?" he asked.

No. But she nodded and forced herself to walk to the bike.

Piper was pretty sure she didn't have any repressed memories of scary rides, but the sound and the size of the machines had frightened her when she was little. When she was older, she'd associated motorcycles with unhappiness and the dread of losing her friends when she and her mother made the inevitable move.

She felt dread creeping through her now, even though Mark had kept up a soothing stream of reassurances and instructions she hoped he'd repeat because she sure wasn't in a state of mind to remember.

He swung his leg over the saddle and for a microscopic instant, Piper understood why bikers had appealed to her mother. The jeans, the boots and the fitted jacket emphasized his leanness and gave him a dangerous air. Not that Mark needed the outfit to look dangerous.

"When you're ready, put your hand on my shoulder, swing your leg over and hop on back."

Right. He'd told her to wear jeans, but he'd also told her they were meeting his friends, so Piper had gone out and bought a new pair of the same brand of jeans Toni had been wearing that day at Friezen Burger.

Not a lot of give in the oh-so-flattering jeans. Piper wasn't going to be hopping anywhere.

"Once you're in place, put your feet on the passenger foot pedals, here." He pointed to little bitty bars that he'd folded out. "Be sure and keep them there because you don't want to burn yourself on the exhaust pipe."

No, she didn't want to burn herself on the exhaust pipe.

Awkwardly, she approached the bike and drew on the gloves. All righty, then. Piece of cake. But as soon as she braced her hand on his shoulder, Mark started the engine and she was hit with a wave of nausea.

No, she couldn't do this. Piper clawed at her helmet, dragging in lungfuls of air as soon as it was off. The exhaust smell didn't help. She backed away.

Mark immediately killed the motor. "What's wrong?"

"I can't." She swallowed, feeling better now that the thing wasn't actually running. "I'm not the motorcycle type." She thrust the helmet at him. "Wait here and I'll follow you in my car." She struggled to pull off the gloves.

"Piper." He spoke calmly and without heat.

"I'm sorry. Don't make me do this." Piper was trying not to look hysterical, while at the same time letting him know she had no intention of getting on his motorcycle.

"I'm not going to make you do anything."

She breathed easier, even though she knew he wouldn't have forced her to ride the bike.

"I do want a favor. And you can say no."

"What?"

"Will you sit behind me? Just while it's parked. I won't even start it up."

He was pulling the desensitizing stuff. Fine, she'd sit on the stupid bike. Always assuming the jeans would allow her to. "Okay. But I'm not putting the helmet back on."

"We're not going anywhere, so you don't need to."

Gingerly, Piper approached him, and with the help of Mark's quiet reminders of where to place her hands and feet, and the miracle of stretch denim, Piper swung her leg over the bike and settled into the saddle behind him. And she did mean settle. The most intimate parts of her body were snug against Mark's hips.

Although he said nothing, she felt him tense. In this position, she could feel everything. Warmth from their bodies permeated her hips and upper thighs. Heat from touching him came from the inside. She wanted to rock against him and let the friction create even more heat. Being able to actually think about something other than being on a motorcycle astounded her. Lifting shaky legs, she propped her feet on the passenger pedals and eased her body away from his a little. Still touching, in places, but not, well, smushed.

"How's that?"

Close. "Well, have you ever ridden behind?"

"Sure, I've been a passenger."

"It's like that."

He laughed.

Maybe it wasn't quite the same. Mentally, she reversed positions with her sitting in front and Mark pressed against her from behind. Yeah. She shivered.

"Are you comfortable?"

Not the word she would use, what with the tight jeans and a hot guy between her thighs. "I don't feel as though we're going to fall over, but we're not moving. And I'm not suggesting that we do," she added hastily.

"It's very steady." Mark had his feet on the ground and moved the bike from side to side.

Piper gasped and grabbed his jacket.

Mark stilled. "You either can use the handgrips, hold my hips or wrap your arms around my abdomen. That makes it easier for me to lean into curves."

She just bet it did.

He started moving the bike gently and bounced a couple of times. Gradually, Piper relaxed her death grip on the hand holds, but grabbed at Mark again when he tilted a little too far to one side.

She figured he was doing it on purpose to encourage her to hold his waist, but Piper wrapped her arms around him anyway.

MARK CLOSED HIS EYES when he felt Piper's arms sneak around his waist and her body relax against his. He savored the sensation, disappointed that it wouldn't last as long as he'd originally planned.

He'd never thought she'd be scared of motorcycles and he'd wanted to share the experience of something he loved with her. Discovering he could still ride had made all the painful months of physical therapy worth it. It wasn't the specter of walking with a limp that drove him; it was the thought of never riding a bike again. Amazing how losing one small chunk of muscle could have such a lasting impact.

He'd been achy this morning and he'd ache tomorrow. He didn't care. He was riding again.

"Thank you," he heard from behind him. "You're very patient."

"No problem."

He heard a sigh. "You can turn on the engine. I know you want to."

His heart beat harder, but he said, "Not unless you're comfortable."

"Ha. I'll never be comfortable, but go ahead. Just don't move!"

"You're not wearing a helmet. My passengers wear helmets." He waited, but when she didn't ask for it back, he started the engine.

"It tickles," he heard and smiled.

It was nice the way they could sit there, engine idling. He didn't have to be somewhere or make some connection or race off to beat the competition for a story. He could just sit and be.

One of Piper's hands slid perilously close to eyebrow raising territory on its way to the helmet he held in his lap. She tugged it and he handed it back to her without asking if she was sure. She was a big girl. If she wasn't sure, she wouldn't be putting on the helmet.

She tapped his shoulder. "Just to the end of the block."

Mark nodded and turned around to check her helmet before easing the bike forward. She tensed, but he kept the speed slow and stopped gently at the end of the block. She pointed to the right and he guessed she was telling him to go around the block, but when he got to the end she pointed left. Still going well under the speed limit, he gently turned, feeling her tense with each movement. They kept going until Piper pointed to a deserted medical center parking lot and Mark knew she wanted to practice.

They remained in the parking lot until Mark felt Piper's body stay relaxed during practice turns, stops and starts.

He pulled beneath a tree and cut the engine. "Where to?"

She drew a breath and said, "Let's go meet your friends— if we're not too late."

He gave her a huge smile, which she couldn't see because not only was she behind him, they were wearing helmets.

Pulling off his gloves, Mark removed his helmet and signaled her to get off the bike, then got off himself.

"What's wrong?" she asked.

"Not a thing." He unsnapped her chin strap and she pulled off the helmet.

Smiling, he gazed into her eyes, knowing she could see everything he felt. "Thank you."

And then he kissed her.

He didn't hold back. This was a barn burner of a kiss. He kissed Piper the way a man kisses a woman who makes him happier when he's with her than when he's not. The way a man kisses a woman who beats back a lifelong fear because she doesn't want to disappoint him. The way a man kisses a woman he's falling for and doesn't care if she knows it.

That kind of kiss.

Piper's cold lips quickly warmed beneath his as she threw her arms around him and kissed him back. Emotions he hadn't allowed himself to feel for a very long time flared to life. Mark drew her close and deepened the kiss. His tongue found hers and he explored her mouth with the same eagerness that she explored his. He tasted sweet passion, but that was the only sweet thing about his kiss.

There was no turning back and she knew it as well as he did. No pretending it didn't happen, not when she was making those little sounds deep in her throat and standing on tiptoe to get closer.

Heat spread through him. He moved his hands against her back wishing the leather jacket he'd lent her didn't fit quite so snugly. But she shifted and his fingers encountered a strip of bare skin above the waistband of her jeans. He stroked it until he felt her laugh through the kiss.

"That tickles," she breathed against his mouth.

"Do you like tickles?" he asked.

"I could. Depends on who's doing the tickling. Or what, 'cause that bike has some seriously good vibrations."

"Oh, Piper." He gripped her in a tight hug, content to hold her close. To cherish her. To let go of that part of himself he always protected because he'd been disappointed so many times. Holding her, he felt an easing within himself. He could relax because she wouldn't hurt him.

And if that didn't scare him, then he was in a lot deeper than he'd suspected. He was sending all kinds of signals here and if he didn't intend to follow through, then he should back off pronto. He should back off, anyway, because they were out in public. Again. Mark smiled and brought his forehead to rest against hers. If they were ever alone when they kissed, it would be incendiary.

"Hey," he whispered and drew back. "Let's go meet my friends."

She nodded and waited while he got on the bike. "Mark? Did you kiss me like that because, well, in case something happens while we're riding and you never get the opportunity?"

She was still scared, then. Mark wished he could wrap her in bubble wrap for this first ride. "No," he assured her. "I did not kiss you because we're about to embark upon a dangerous journey from which we might not return."

"You're laughing at me," she grumbled as she put on her helmet. By herself.

"I'm trying hard not to laugh. No, I kissed you because…" Belatedly, he realized he shouldn't have started the sentence until he knew the answer.

"Because…?"

Because I'm falling in love with you. But he couldn't say that. Not before walking away in a few weeks. He stared down at her. "For the same reason you kissed me back."

She fastened her chin strap. "That's a good reason." She put her hand on his shoulder and got on behind him, wiggled around some and wound her arms around his waist. "Let's go!"

"This is Chip and this is Lexie." Mark bent down and patted the heads of two largish mixed breed dogs. "Did you two think I'd forgotten you? I'd never forget you."

"Man's best friend. Very clever," Piper said.

Her first motorcycle ride had ended with yet another surprise when Mark pulled into a no-kill animal shelter. "I come here and play with the dogs," he told her. "They need to get out and interact with humans. It's good exercise for me, too. Working my leg on machines is one thing, but I need to test it with real-life twists and turns." He was squatting by the animals, who'd both rolled over so he could scratch their bellies. "Good dog," he murmured repeatedly, allocating one hand to each. "They just want to be loved. Their people abandoned them and they don't know what they did wrong." He rubbed their necks and scratched behind their ears.

"Are you talking about yourself or the dogs?" she asked.

"Let's just say I know how they feel." He looked up at her with those blue eyes she could lose herself in. "Do you like dogs?"

He probably asked because she hadn't petted them or anything. "I don't know. We didn't have pets." She watched him move his hands over the dogs, who were still panting from their joyous run to greet him. "I don't dislike them," she added.

He gestured. "Pet the nice doggies, Piper."

She knelt beside him and rubbed a tummy. That earned her a lick and not from Mark.

"Chip likes you. He's got good taste."

"Or maybe I just taste good."

"That, too." Mark's eyes darkened and Piper knew he was remembering. She was remembering, too. For several seconds, they gazed at each other, and then looked away.

They petted the dogs in silence. Piper stole a glance at Mark. He seemed as happy to see the dogs as they were to see him. A cynical part of her pointed out that he could be trying to make himself look good, but why would he bother? No. Just look at his unguarded face and relaxed body. This was the real deal. The real Mark sharing something with her.

And she fell just a little more in love with him because of it, darn it. How did Dancie think this was going to help her? Was she supposed to rank "loves dogs" higher on her perfect man compatibility questionnaire?

Finally Piper asked, "Why did you bring me here?"

Mark smiled to himself before glancing at her. "A date?"

She blinked at him. "It is?"

He winced. "As we've discussed, I don't 'date,' but I thought an afternoon ride and a stop here would be better than conversational ping-pong over dinner."

"It is!" Surprisingly, even with the shock of actually riding a motorcycle, she meant it. "But usually, there's a heads-up."

"You mean like, oh, say, a hot kiss in a parking lot?" His gaze dropped to her mouth.

"Well, yes." She concentrated on picking bits of grass out of Chip's fur. "But I meant something before the actual date begins. I thought you wanted to discuss the last group you interviewed."

He scratched behind Lexie's ears. "Nothing to discuss."

"There is, since you keep rejecting everyone." Chip nosed her hand because she'd stopped petting him, so she patted his head and rubbed his tummy again. "You just want attention, don't you?" She looked up at Mark. "Both of you."

"Hey."

"Well? When are you going to stop rejecting everyone I send you?" Piper asked.

"When are you going to send me the person you really recommend?"

"I recommended them all!"

He shook his head. "When you find the right person, you won't hide her in a group."

Busted. "I didn't want to take a chance that you'd reject her just because you're trying to make a point."

"And what point would I be making?"

"That you're Mark Banning, important world-famous journalist. You don't want to work with anyone and since you're being forced to, you're not going to make it easy. You want BT to realize that not just anyone will be good enough."

"True," he readily admitted. "But if there had been a real standout, I would have approved her."

Piper tilted her head and squinted at him. "Really?"

He squinted back. "I like to think so."

"Okay, because I actually have two I think are equally good, but in different ways." Piper told him a little about them. "Frankly, Mark, if you can't work with either of these two, then it's because you don't *want* to work with them."

He nodded. "Fair enough."

Lexie stretched and rolled over. "Maybe I should just take Lexie with me. You'd like to work with me, wouldn't you, Lexie?"

Lexie's ears perked up and he smiled. "This is why I like

coming here. The dogs don't care about any of those games. They don't know if you're famous or rich or rule a small country. You can't pretend with dogs. You're just you and they either like you or they don't."

He gave her a quick sideways look. "You remind me of them. I guess that's why I wanted to bring you here."

Piper took in Chip's tangled blond fur and self-consciously touched the windblown bits of hers that the helmet hadn't covered. "Lovely."

"You are." He smiled at her, holding her gaze. "You're a lovely person."

Piper's hand slid slowly back to her lap. That may have been the best compliment she'd ever been given. It wasn't something she'd expect a man of his type to say. But he wasn't acting like a man of his type.

"When I said you remind me of these guys, I meant that you never paid any attention to the man I was supposed to be. You wanted to know the man I am." He looked back at the dogs. "You might know me better than I do."

"Everybody has a public and a private self, Mark. Yours aren't as far apart as you think they are."

"Yours are."

"What?" Sure, she had a normal amount of reserve, but she wasn't the one with a whole different persona.

But Mark was nodding. "You have this whole, blank mask thing going." He gestured around his face. "And you have these intense, all-seeing scientist eyes that are always analyzing."

"I do not!"

"Yes. And this flat voice—it's scary." He gave a mock shudder.

Piper was laughing. "It's not that bad! I'm trying to look neutral and nonjudgmental."

"You look robotic. It wasn't until you got mad at me that I knew you had any emotions at all."

"I have lots of emotions," she protested.

"Which I am very much interested in sharing with you."

As he leaned forward and kissed her, Piper thought, *Yeah, me, too.*

It was a kiss full of sensual promise to which she'd responded with an enthusiasm he couldn't possibly miss. Yeah, her body took over and gave him the green light. A bright, flashing green light with arrows pointing the way and a marching band ready to welcome him.

This was not her style, but as Dancie had recently pointed out, her style wasn't working for her.

Dancie had told her she needed to find out what attracted her to him. What didn't?

She was really, really past hope. Her defenses were gone. Her sense of self-preservation had evaporated. After the kiss in the parking lot, and forty-five nerve-racking minutes spent with her arms wrapped around him while being hyperaware of every move of his body, she knew where this was going. It was only a matter of when, where and how often.

A couple of wet dog noses nudged at them and they laughed.

"I know, I know. Time to play ball, right?" Mark got to his feet and held out his hand to help Piper up. "Usually, I'm by myself, so I have to work into a rhythm where one dog chases a ball as the other brings one back to me."

She watched as he played with the dogs and laughed because she'd throw the icky ball, covered in dog slobber, but the dogs would always return it to Mark.

Piper noticed that he wasn't the only volunteer to play with the animals, but he was the best-looking, if she did say so herself.

The rest of the afternoon was a lot of fun. Piper didn't associate fun with Mark—another surprise. She thought she had him all figured out, but the more they talked and the more she discovered about him, the more she wondered if her Piper

Plan was totally bogus. Because how could it describe her perfect man as anyone other than Mark?

So when they arrived back at her apartment, only the repeated buzz of Mark's cell phone kept his goodbye kiss from becoming a let's-continue-this-inside kiss.

She knew he would have ignored the phone, but the thing was buzzing against her ribs. "Maybe it's important."

"Not as important as you," he said.

"Now, that's a good line. Keep that one."

He lowered his head. "I'd rather keep—"

She laughed. "Check your phone!"

She felt Mark tense when he stared at the caller's number and knew she'd been right to insist.

"Piper, I—"

"It's okay. Go."

With an apologetic smile, he kissed her on the forehead, and left.

Piper was grateful for the reprieve. Frustrated, but grateful.

There was something she needed to do, anyway. Letting herself into her apartment, she flipped on the light and took her phone into the kitchen. After pouring herself a glass of wine, she sat down and made a call. "Hello, Mom."

"Piper! Hey, look. I know I owe you money, but if you can wait a couple of weeks—"

"I'm not calling about the money."

"What's wrong?" Her mother's voice changed, becoming, well, more motherly.

"Mom…I'm about to do something really stupid."

11

Step eleven: Is the man you want the man you need?

IT HAD BEEN A PERFECT DAY and would have been a perfect night, as well. But Mark's phone had buzzed with three calls one after another—while he was kissing Piper. He needed to see who was calling. But only a total jerk would interrupt a kiss to check his cell. There was no acceptable way to say "Hang on and I'll get back to you." It was barely okay to end it the way he had, and he'd only done so because he'd sensed her hesitation.

She was right. It was better that they step back now and think, rather than act and have regrets. He could be patient.

The irony was not lost on him.

After Mark left Piper, he'd ridden a little way down the street before pulling over and checking the call log. So he hadn't imagined the number.

His stomach roiled as he remembered the months he'd spent as a captive with Mendoza, the low-life Mexican drug trafficker.

Mark had programmed his private number into a prepaid cell phone and given it to Hector, the younger brother of Gilberto, one of the boys Mendoza had tried to recruit. He'd told

Hector to call if he or Gilberto got into trouble. Mark had been writing a story on children used to transport drugs. When Mendoza discovered it, he'd kidnapped those who'd talked to him. Everyone, which told Mark that someone had betrayed them. And him. He never found out who.

That had been a year and a half ago and he was surprised the batteries in the phone still worked. He returned the call, and instead of Hector, Mendoza, himself, had answered. Truthfully, Mark wasn't all that surprised.

"Mark, my friend," Mendoza greeted him heartily.

Mark thought of Piper and the way she detached herself from her emotions so she could analyze a situation. He wished she was listening in now. "I'm not your friend."

"But we have many friends in common. They're here with me. Say hello to Mark, *mis amigos*."

Mark squeezed his eyes shut as several young voices called out in the background. He couldn't tell how many. Enough.

"See? They are still your friends, even though you have broken your promise to return."

Not yet, he hadn't.

"My heart, it hurts to see them wait for so long. I explain to them you are an important man. A busy man. It is understandable that such a man would forget them. They tell me 'No. Senor Mark, he would not forget us.'"

Mark could hear murmuring in the background. Mendoza liked to pretend he was an unsophisticated, common man who did what he had to do to survive. In reality, he was university educated, came from an urban, upper-middle-class background and was a shrewd manipulator. He also spoke perfect English.

"So, Senor Mark, did you forget them?"

Mark struggled to keep his voice free of all the hate and disgust he felt for this man. "What do you want?"

Mendoza laughed lightly. "I have not decided. It would depend on what you are willing to pay."

Mark remained silent.

Mendoza spoke away from the handset. "Hector, my little friend, you told me he would help you. It seems you lied."

"No!" Mark heard. It might have been Hector or not. For Mendoza's purposes, it didn't matter.

"You know what we do to liars."

"But he told me! Senor Mark, please!"

The boy spoke in English and the whole thing was no doubt scripted for Mark's benefit, but the sound of flesh being hit was real enough.

"You can stop," he said into the phone. "You've made your point."

"Have I?" Mendoza asked. "Because you do not sound convinced."

Maybe he was channeling Piper too well. "You want something from me and if I give it to you, you will release the boys." He would have added *unharmed,* but Mendoza would use it as a negotiating tool against him. "I'm waiting to hear what that something is."

There was silence and then, "I will contact you." Mendoza disconnected.

Mark had always intended to return to the Texas-Mexico border and finish the story by eliminating Mendoza, but he'd planned to go after generating some goodwill with BT and ratings for Travis. He'd been off the air for too long to have the clout he needed, never mind the financial backing. But Mendoza wouldn't know that. The last time he'd seen Mark, he was being carried off by well-armed, highly effective private mercenaries.

Mark had a hunch that whatever Mendoza wanted had to do with them.

For the first time, he was glad BT had insisted that he start working with someone. Because right now, Mark could sure use the help.

PIPER LISTENED INCREDULOUSLY as one of her top choices for Mark filled her in on her interview. "Let me make sure I heard you correctly—you're saying Mark refused to hire you because you wouldn't sleep with him?" Piper's voice brought both Dancie and Anna running to her office even though they could hear her half of the conversation perfectly well from the reception area.

Of course, Shelley, the attractive woman in her mid-thirties with the six siblings, was so irate, they could hear her voice through the phone, as well. "Are you positive you didn't misunderstand?"

"It's hard to misunderstand 'I need you to sleep with me so I can see if we're compatible.' Sorry, but no. I stopped sleeping with interviewers to get jobs a long time ago."

Dancie's eyes widened and Anna clapped her hand over her mouth.

Piper struggled for composure. "I'm going to speak with him and—"

"Ask Mary Wade. She was there."

Mary was Piper's other top pick.

"He told her he couldn't hire her because she had kids. That was right before he said he needed to sleep with me."

"I apologize, Shelley." Although she was positive Shelley had misunderstood. "I assure you, I will discuss this with him."

After hanging up, she, Dancie and Anna stared at each other.

"Sounds like Mark," Dancie said at the same time Piper said, "That does *not* sound like Mark."

"I don't know Mark," Anna said. "And I don't want to."

Piper called Mary Wade, who confirmed Shelley's story and added that they'd been at Mark's home doing research for him as a test. Stunned, Piper apologized again.

"I can't believe this." She looked up at Dancie. "I thought he was…" *Different,* she'd been going to say. But he'd just played her the way he played everyone. She hadn't fallen for the heroic adventurer routine, so he'd shown her a vulnerable man who needed love.

A vulnerable man who needs love. "He went to my website." She started typing on her laptop.

"Excuse me, there's nothing on your site that condones sexual harassment," Dancie said.

"Not that." Piper brought up the personality grid and read part of the alpha-alpha description out loud. "'The heroic, demanding, leadership characteristics frequently mask a past trauma and/or loneliness. At his core, the alpha-alpha is a vulnerable man who needs love.'" She gritted her teeth and went on, "'He considers it a weakness and will rarely, if ever, reveal it.'" Piper felt nauseous.

"What does that mean?" Anna asked.

"It means he showed her his vulnerable side," Dancie told her.

Nodding, Piper closed her laptop. "He fed me little bits and pieces of his past. I swear, it was like catnip."

"I take back what I said about getting involved with Mark," Dancie said. "Big mistake."

Piper gave her a brittle smile. "Too late."

"*Actually* too late or *thinking about it* too late?" Dancie asked.

Piper yanked open the file drawer where she kept her purse. "*He'll wish we'd never met* too late."

"THANKS FOR THE INFO." Mark ended the phone call and made a note, one of many he'd scribbled since hearing from Mendoza yesterday. Strewn across his dining room table were old files and notes, maps and printouts from flash drives, and transcriptions of electronic memos.

While he had everything scanned and backed up electronically, he preferred seeing all his information at once.

Mark studied the wall-size topographical map of the

Texas-Mexico border he'd tacked to his dining room wall, and zeroed in on an area near Big Bend State Park. Since Mark's escape, Mendoza had moved his main headquarters but still took advantage of the wilderness on the edges of the park and its proximity to the border.

After spending months in Mendoza's remote camp, Mark knew how the man thought, what elements he looked to exploit and his favorite methods. All Mark needed was a general area where Mendoza's people had been seen to figure out where he was holed up.

His doorbell rang and someone pounded on the door at the same time. The way Mark's luck had been running, it would probably be the boyfriend of that nutcase woman who'd thought he was hitting on her.

Mark quietly approached the door and took the precaution of checking the peephole.

A thin-lipped Piper glared straight at it.

And when he opened the door, she glared at him.

"Piper!" She was angry, but why? True, he hadn't called her after abruptly leaving last night, but it hadn't even been twenty-four hours since he'd seen her. And he'd been busy, working flat-out, thinking of nothing but finding Mendoza and taking him out. But he knew better than to say so.

"Oh, you remember me?"

Okay, he should have called her. "Sorry I haven't called yet, but things got a little crazy."

"I heard they got a lot crazy. May I come in?" She tried to look around him. "Or do you already have someone in your lair?"

"No, my lair is at your disposal."

She swept past him. "Ha!"

Ha? What did that mean?

Instead of enlightening him, she was walking the perimeter of his living room where he'd hung dozens of black-framed photographs of people he'd met on past assignments. He was in most of them, as well. If he could, Mark gave the subjects a copy as a little memento.

But Piper wasn't here to look at his pictures.

She was still dressed in her "seeing client" clothes—a plain skirt and a top. She wore boots and held her shoulder bag—not the ugly one with the camera—close to her body. She might have been an art gallery patron.

When the minutes passed and she didn't say anything, Mark decided to ask, "What's wrong?"

Wheeling around, she planted herself in front of him and demanded, "Did you or did you not tell Shelley she had to sleep with you before you'd hire her?"

Mark grimaced. The nutcase. "I can explain."

"I'm sure you can," she snapped. "Yes or no?"

"Yes. But—"

"How *could* you?" Anger radiated from her. She was no longer the emotionally detached professional Mark saw most of the time. Her face was flushed and her eyes glittered with emotion.

Now, that's *passion,* he thought, when he should have been explaining.

"How could you kiss me the way you did and then turn around and ask another woman to sleep with you?" Her chest heaved and the hand that gripped her purse strap quivered.

"I said 'sleep,' not have sex." Slowly it dawned on Mark that Piper had acted before getting all the facts. He'd had some experience with impulsiveness, but for her, this was way out of character.

"That does not make it okay!" She glared at him. "I rode a motorcycle for you! You introduced me to abandoned dogs! You told me about your mother!" She'd been stepping forward as she spoke and now she jabbed a finger at him. "You made me fall for you!"

Mark keyed in on the important info. "You've fallen for me?"

"Don't act surprised. You're the master manipulator. Poor,

vulnerable, love-starved man. I didn't have a chance, did I?"
She looked up at the ceiling. "How could I have been so stupid? Stupid, stupid, stupid."

A slow smile spread across Mark's face. "You're jealous!"

He started to tell her that not only didn't she need to feel jealous, but that he'd pretty much fallen for her, too, when, with an impressively primal roar of frustration, Piper raised her fist.

Mark caught it in his hand.

They stared at each other and then Piper gasped. "Look what you made me do! You made me want to *hit* something. Hit *you!*" She tugged. "Give me back my hand!"

"No way." Mark shook his head.

"Why? Because you want me to *calm down* first?"

He nodded.

"Don't tell me to calm down!" She jerked her arm once more, knocking them both off balance. They collided, chest to chest, breathing heavily.

One of them should back up. It wasn't going to be Mark.

Piper's warm body was pressed against him and her face was inches from his. They weren't on a sidewalk, in a parking lot or in a field with dogs. They were alone. He could kiss her for as long as he wanted, the way he wanted and where he wanted. Desire burned within him. It wasn't the hot flare he was used to, but a slow, steady heat that would last a long time. Gazing into her angry face, Mark knew Piper was the one woman who could make him forget everything else. No, worse than that, he wouldn't forget. He would no longer care.

Piper stared at him, and then she sagged. "Listen to me! I sound like an escapee from a reality TV show!"

He nodded. "Little bit."

She inhaled and exhaled, looking off to the side, struggling to regain her composure. There wasn't much left to regain. "I can't believe you propositioned that woman. Not only is it illegal, it's tacky."

She sounded more like herself, so Mark figured it was safe to explain. "Come with me." Uncurling her fist, he laced their fingers together and drew her into his bedroom.

"You are kidding," Piper protested. "Even your ego can't be so big that you think I'd... Why is there a tent in your bedroom?"

PIPER WASN'T TALKING about a romantic, white canopy enveloping the bed in gauzy fabric, either. This was a small, mud-colored tent. On the floor.

"If I know I'm going on assignment into a remote area, I acclimate myself by sleeping on the floor in the sleeping bag I plan to take with me," Mark told her. "I also go backpacking, especially when I need to check out new equipment. This is all new, since my old stuff didn't make it out of Mexico with me."

"Oh." That was all Piper could manage. She was emotionally drained, and really, what else was there to say to Mark's perfectly reasonable explanation for pitching a tent in his bedroom?

"I've followed stories into some remote areas and it's only possible because I've prepared for it. Even in towns, there are times I end up sleeping outside in someone's yard or barn, or a bombed-out building. Sometimes I sleep with my contacts on the floor of their house." He spoke matter-of-factly. Calmly. As though he were speaking to a hysterical person who was about to realize she'd made a huge error in coming to his house and yelling at him.

"And it's rare," he continued, "but it happens that I also get to sleep on silk sheets in palaces."

"That would be my first choice."

Mark raised his eyebrows. "Believe it or not, I actually feel safer sleeping on someone's floor."

"Why?"

"It's easier to avoid political intrigue."

He sounded as though he was giving a tour of his home to a casual acquaintance and not someone he'd taken motorcycle riding and then kissed until her lips were numb. Someone who then appeared on his doorstep the next evening accusing him of propositioning another woman.

She had lost it. Completely lost it. He was the one who'd remained calm and detached and was now allowing her to get ahold of herself. How utterly embarrassing.

"So would you say you spend as much time roughing it as you do in hotels?" Oh, listen to her, all calm and professional, and not like someone who had recently accused him of sexual harassment and emotional manipulation.

Laughing, he said, "Some of the hotels where I've stayed would be considered 'roughing it' by our standards. But I know what you're asking. Honestly, I prefer getting close to my subjects, so I end up staying in hotels only about a quarter to a third of the time."

"Really?" This was information she should have known.

He nodded. "When you get out of that Western bubble and get to know the people, see how they live, and eat their food, you can't help but learn more."

"Like method acting," she said. "You're a method journalist."

"Method journalist. I like that." He smiled down at her and rubbed his thumb across hers.

Yeah, he still held her hand. Piper managed a sickly smile back as she recalled telling him she'd fallen for him.

This was excruciating. He was being nice about it and *nice* wasn't a word associated with Mark, which made her embarrassment worse.

He gestured to the items propped against the wall. "That's my travel gear. I carry everything with me so I don't have to go back for luggage. That includes this two-man pup tent." Mark nudged it with his foot. "Because I've never traveled with anyone, I don't know if it will actually be practical for two people and their gear, or if we'll need a second tent. And there's only one way to find out."

"Oh, I know where this is going." Piper sighed as she realized what had happened with Shelley. "You need two people to test it."

"Exactly."

"Why not just assume your partner will need her own tent?"

"It'll be extra weight for her to carry around. But even then, there will be times when I won't want her out of sight. It's never a good situation when a lone woman is around men who've been away from their families for a very long time."

"I see." Piper wished they'd had this conversation before she started screening candidates. And they would have if she hadn't canceled it because she was so unnerved after practically attacking him the day they'd walked back from Friezen's. "BT can't fully understand what the circumstances are like or he wouldn't insist that you take a woman with you. It would be asking a lot of anyone, man or woman."

"We'll be living with each other day and night. I could never hire anyone without first going on a dry run to see how she handles it," Mark said.

"Maybe you should take BT backpacking."

"Not a bad idea." He smiled down at her.

Her heart caught. He wasn't even trying and she could feel herself go all mushy. "Why didn't you tell Shelley this?"

"I did. Almost verbatim. But she had a preconception about me and couldn't get past it."

"Are we talking about the Mark Banning reputation with the ladies?"

The smile disappeared. "We're talking about a journalist who based her assumptions on hearsay, not fact. That's unacceptable."

"I'll explain everything to her." Piper wished she felt better now that she knew Mark didn't have a journalist's version of the casting couch, except she'd done a little conclusion jumping, herself.

"I'd appreciate it." He rubbed the back of his head. "She's not taking my calls and I don't want to get sued. But she's definitely out of the running."

Piper nodded. And as long as they were clearing things up... "Mary Wade? Is it true that you rejected her because she has kids?"

"Yes." His expression became grim and implacable. "We'll be gone for weeks at a time. I'm not going to be responsible for separating a mother from her children."

"One is in college and the other two are teenagers," she agreed.

"*Young* teens. I lived through that and I won't do it to other kids." There was more anger in his voice now than when she'd been ranting.

"It's not the same as your situation," Piper said gently. "Their father—"

"It's not negotiable."

"Okay." Piper backed off. "But I really hoped it would be a way for her to get back into journalism."

"You don't have to worry about her," Mark said. "She's very talented. There's a guy I owe in Arizona—Wally—who runs a regional bureau. I recommended Mary to him."

"You did? That was so...nice of you!" And unexpected. Almost saintly.

Piper felt really horrible now.

"Eh." He shrugged it off. "Now and then I do the odd good deed."

"This good deed leaves you without a partner. We have to start all over. That's assuming you still want me to work with you after the way I've acted." Battling past the embarrassment, Piper forced herself to meet his eyes. There was no anger, no disgust. He looked...happy?

"Why wouldn't I?"

"Because! I got all upset and barged into your home—"

"You called it a 'lair.'" His mouth twitched. The man was laughing at her.

"I am so sorry. I have no excuse. I knew there had to be a reasonable explanation for what you said, but I...I just snapped."

"You were jealous." Mark turned to face her and pulled her hand around his waist.

"I was not! I was incensed on behalf of a client."

He looped his arms around her. "You were hair-pulling, face-scratching, cat-fighting jealous."

It was true. Horribly true. She'd never felt that way in her entire life. Until a second ago, he'd been holding the hand she'd raised to hit him. Truly, there was no apology that would ever negate that, but she had to try. "I—"

Mark swooped down and captured her mouth with his.

And that was pretty much it for Piper. She let go of everything—caution, self-preservation, common sense. Her heart. She let it all go and felt an overwhelming relief now that she wasn't struggling to hold back. She wanted to tell him how she felt, but her mouth was busy being kissed three ways to Sunday.

From the way she was kissing him back, he probably knew, anyway.

Mark tugged them closer until their bodies were pressed tightly together and it still wasn't close enough.

She wanted touching. Lots and lots of touching. She needed skin. Piper jerked his shirt from the waistband of his jeans and ran her hands over his back. When he held her tighter, she felt the muscles move beneath the taut skin. He was such a *man*. A take-charge, no-holds-barred man. Way higher up the testosterone scale than the perfect man she wanted. But Mark was exactly the man she needed.

Lifting his mouth a whisper away from hers, he said, "I'm

falling for you, you're falling for me—don't you think it's time we catch each other?"

She smiled, lips tingling. "Still with the cheesy lines."

He bent and before Piper realized what he was doing, he'd caught her behind the knees and picked her up. "I've got cheesy moves, too."

Piper laughed. "Wanna know a secret?"

"I want to know all your secrets."

"I kind of like your cheesy lines."

"What about my move, here?"

Piper had to admit that there was a lot of appeal being held in a man's strong arms. She settled her head against his chest where his heart thumped against her cheek. "I like it, too."

She felt a quiver and he swayed as he shifted weight. He took a step that felt more like necessity than design.

"Your leg?"

"Not yet, but in attempting to sweep you off your feet, I failed to consider the dismount. Might be a tough landing."

"Where were you sweeping me to?"

"My tent."

"Why? Were you thinking *Lawrence of Arabia?*" Piper stared at the small tent, and the hard floor beneath the small tent.

"I was thinking *prone and naked.* I figured I'd work out the details as I went along."

"Typical."

He shifted her in his arms and took another step.

"You said the tent was for sleeping."

"I did."

She nipped the corner of his mouth. "But I'm not sleepy."

"Neither am I."

Mark swept her around the tent to the bed he'd shoved into the corner. And, yes, the sweeping was more of a lurching and the dismount was a little bouncy, but Mark displayed an impressive talent with zippers and buttons. Piper had more motivation than talent, and after pulling Mark's shirt over his head, she was highly motivated.

"I've… I've never actually seen a six-pack in person before." Pretty intimidating for someone who'd been hitting the carbs lately. She sucked in her stomach as Mark worked her skirt over her hips.

"Physical therapy—it's not just for legs," he said, and his breath tickled her stomach.

She gave a short gasp and he paused, eyebrow raised. She read the intent in his eyes and distracted him by reaching for his zipper. And then she became distracted by the bulge behind the zipper.

Mark had been on his knees and straightened, so she was now eye to eye, or more accurately, eye to bulge.

Here was the thing: Piper hadn't encountered all that many bulges in her life and she didn't remember them being quite so…bulgy. She did remember that men were wary of zippers in that area. Before she did any unzipping, she needed to get the lay of the land, so to speak. A little topographical exploration.

Her fingers lightly stroked the firm mound beneath the zipper and were tracing down his thigh when Mark's hand clamped over her wrist and he moved her fingers away.

She looked to his face to see what was wrong and saw his chest heave as he breathed deeply. "You—you better let me." He released her wrist.

"I was going to be careful."

He gave a short laugh. "It's not that." He focused on a place over her head and swallowed. "It's been a long time. A really long time." Looking back at her, he grinned crookedly. "And I really want you."

She understood. "Same here." Although his idea of a long time was probably not the same as hers. "I've been waiting and waiting to just *feel* something for a man again, and now that I do, I'm done with waiting." Piper let her breath out in a whoosh. "So please, please tell me you've got a condom."

"I do." He hesitated. "Somewhere."

"I've never known a man who didn't know exactly where the condoms were."

He glanced over his shoulder at the equipment lining the wall next to the tent. "Like I said, long time."

Piper shimmied her skirt the rest of the way off. "Maybe this will jog your memory." She tossed it on the floor next to her top.

Mark stared down at her, his eyes darkening. "I've had dreams about your skin. The wig made it look so white that day. All I could see was your face, your neck and your hands, but I dreamed about your body." His voice deepened. "I drove myself crazy wondering if your nipples would be brown or pink."

Piper's brownish-pink nipples tightened inside her bra. "If you ever want to know, you'd better find those condoms."

He stood and started unbuckling his belt. When the zipper rasped, Piper closed her eyes before she did something truly reckless, like telling him to forget the condoms. Leaving her was one thing, leaving her with a child to raise, to remind her of him every day for the rest of her life, was unthinkable.

There was a clang as his jeans and belt hit the floor. Piper felt the side of the bed sink as he sat. When he didn't move, she opened her eyes and was greeted with a broad expanse of back as he leaned over and searched beneath the bed.

Then he sat up, flashed her a victory grin and showed her the box before dropping it beside the bed.

"Maybe you should keep that a little closer," she told him as he reached for her.

He deftly removed her bra. "Perfect." He smiled. "Absolutely perfect." His smile dazzled her and Piper didn't even care because her brain and her hormones were finally in sync. And when they synced, they really synced.

There was a gorgeous, naked man sitting next to her. And from what she could see, he wanted her. However, the gorgeous, naked man was not moving.

She arched her back inviting him to *touch* her already and felt a whisper of coolness. While she'd been dazzled, he'd removed her panties. But not her boots.

This wasn't actually Piper's style, but judging from the way Mark was looking at her, she was going to make it her style. She lifted her arms above her head and stretched, giving him a sultry look.

His hot gaze traveled over her body, warming her wherever it touched. When she actually felt his hands on her, she'd probably explode.

Her nipples—the same nipples he'd been so anxious to see—were hard and needed his caress.

What was he waiting for? She lowered her arms and slid her hands down her body. As her palms passed over her nipples, a tiny moan escaped.

He inhaled sharply and retrieved the box of condoms. "You're right. We'll need these soon."

He stretched out beside her and Piper's mouth went a little dry. *This is the man,* she thought. *My perfect man.*

"Let me," he murmured, and nudged her arms aside. When she finally felt the warmth of his hands as they held her breasts, she actually shuddered.

His thumbs passed over her nipples and Piper's arms flailed before clutching at his shoulders. Was it too soon to beg?

Mark leaned toward her and took one of her nipples into his mouth. It felt like fireworks going off in her body. Her hips bucked and Piper went mindless with need.

She ran her hands over his back and squirmed beneath him. He flinched and she dragged his head from her breast. "Are you holding back?" She panted between the words.

"Trying to."

"Don't."

His gaze locked on hers and she saw the banked desire. "Don't," she repeated. Then she placed a hand on either side of his face and kissed him.

She made it a demanding kiss and what she was demanding was immediate satisfaction. Right now, she wanted to forget the fancy stuff and not worry about technique. Just the basics. Slow and sensual could wait. She couldn't.

Mark got the message and stopped holding back. He possessed her mouth in a way no man ever had. Mark had an exquisite command of the basics.

His naked desire fed hers and Piper responded on a level she didn't know existed. And couldn't control.

His hands and mouth were everywhere, but it wasn't enough. Her movements grew frantic as she tried to get closer. Something elemental was driving her beyond the pleasure. She wrapped her legs around him, heedless of whether the heels of the boots dug into his back or not.

She felt his muscles bunch and he raised his head, eyes glazed with passion.

"Piper."

She saw his lips move, but heard nothing as she concentrated on the sensation as he slid into her. For a moment, she savored feeling full and complete. Mated. And then he began to move. She spasmed around him almost instantly, gasping his name in surprise. But instead of feeling relief and enjoying waning ripples of pleasure, as Mark drove harder and faster, the ripples gathered into a wave that crashed as he thrust a final time.

They lay there, trying to drag enough air into their lungs. For a while, Piper was conscious of nothing but the sound of their breathing. Then she became aware that they were breathing in the same rhythm. Turning her head, she opened her eyes and saw Mark's face next to hers. He was watching her and she knew he heard it, too.

"Wow," she said.

"Wow is right." He brushed her hair away from her eyes. "I promise you I usually last longer."

"I couldn't have stood longer."

"Hey. You don't have to spare my feelings."

"Are you kidding? I barely kept from passing out."

"Yeah?" He got that satisfied male grin on his face.

"Men." She rolled her eyes.

He shifted and she was aware that her boots were practically embedded in his back. "Oh, sorry!" She moved her legs and winced at the red marks the heels had left. "Did they hurt you?"

"What?" He glanced over his shoulder.

"The boots."

"Oh, yeah, the boots." He rolled over and smiled. "Loved the boots."

12

Step twelve: All men have flaws. Decide which ones you can live with.

THE BOOTS WEREN'T the only thing Mark loved. He suspected he loved Piper, too. Did he know for sure? No. But he wanted to find out.

Piper laughed. "You may change your mind." She sat up and unzipped the boots.

"Nah." Mark absently ran his hand up and down her spine.

He hadn't let himself love for a very long time. He cared; he liked, but he never got love right.

Piper pulled off the boots and her socks. When she leaned across Mark to drop them over the side of the bed, she got a good look at his injured leg.

"Mark!"

He gazed down his body. It looked like something had taken a bite out of the area above his knee. Scars of various shades of pink decorated it. A few inches above that was a scar with suture marks on either side. "Ugly, huh?"

"Who cares about the way it looks? It's what you went through."

"That was ugly, too." He shifted to a sitting position and leaned against the wall.

She scooted up the bed and rested her head against his chest. His arm automatically went around her.

"Tell me."

He'd known she'd ask eventually. "I got shot when I tried to escape and the wound became infected."

"Like your wrist."

"More. There I was, surrounded by drugs of every kind—except antibiotics. By the time they gave me some, the pills weren't strong enough. I was in pretty bad shape when they finally got a doctor to see me." Mark had been delirious and didn't remember. He assumed the man had been a doctor. Maybe not. He skipped that part. "When I got back, I had more surgeries." He pointed. "I'm working to develop this muscle to compensate for the part that's missing."

Piper traced her finger over the higher scar. "How did you get stabbed?"

"During the rescue. Couldn't move out of the way fast enough."

She sat up and he missed the warmth where she'd been nestled against him. As she bent over his knee for a closer look, her hair swung forward and brushed his thigh. That was all it took for things to get stirring again. That, and looking at the curve of her breasts.

She set her palm lightly on his leg. "It's warm. You probably strained it." She smiled over her shoulder. "Next time, I'll be on top."

"I DIDN'T KNOW FRIEZEN BURGER delivered." Piper dipped a fry in queso.

"Officially, they don't," Mark said.

Which meant he'd sweet-talked some poor student into bringing him the order. Piper decided to let it pass and fed him the fry. He ate it and then nibbled on her fingers, making her giggle.

They were in the pup tent with Mark's new sleeping bag unzipped all the way and spread out.

Mark's new sleeping bag smelled like sex now.

And French fries.

"My turn." He dipped a fry in a creamy artichoke sauce and traced a squiggle across her stomach. Then he followed the path with his tongue. And then he ate the fry.

Piper laughed. "That was supposed to be mine!"

"You're insatiable when it comes to French fries."

"And you're insatiable when it comes to sex. Exactly how long had it been?"

Mark popped a naked French fry into her mouth. "Since right before I became Mendoza's guest."

Piper thought back. "You mean…like over a year and a half ago?"

"Don't look at me that way. I was a prisoner for five months. When I got back, my body needed to focus on healing."

"It did a good job," she told him.

Grinning, he fed her another fry. "It did a great job."

Piper nodded her agreement and then asked casually, "There's a picture of a woman and two boys on the wall between the map and the table. Is that her?" She looked right at him to gauge his reaction.

"Yes." He didn't pretend to misunderstand. "How did you know?"

"There aren't any other pictures around it." Piper was curious, not jealous. Yet.

Mark tossed the fry he'd been going to dip and rolled onto his back. Staring at the tent ceiling, he said, "It's there because of her sons, Gilberto and Hector. I'd been in the area a few weeks working on the Mendoza story. He takes boys to use as his couriers. He terrorizes the families, and the local police don't do anything. I wanted to attract media attention so they'd be forced to deal with him. Very few people would talk to me until I met Gilberto one day. I got to know him and his mom and Hector. Elia asked for my help because her brother was pressuring Gilberto to join one of Mendoza's squads. That's when I learned Mendoza paid the boys' families. It's a poor area. No wonder no one wanted to talk to me. I learned a lot from Gilberto because he talked to his friends who were working for Mendoza. And then one day he was gone. Elia was frantic, so I said I would get him back."

"And she was very grateful," Piper said.

"Yep."

There was more he wasn't telling her, but she could guess the rest. "How did you think you could get him back? You're a journalist, not a superhero."

"I had a plan."

"Only it didn't work."

"Oh, it worked."

But he stared, stone-faced, at the tent ceiling, and Piper knew what he'd done. "Mark Banning, you did not offer yourself as a hostage in exchange, did you?"

He rolled to his side and looked at her. "The plan was that several men from the village would trade me for their sons. Then when the boys were safely out, the men were supposed to sneak back for me. I guess they forgot that part."

She heard the bitterness he tried to hide. "Maybe they tried and couldn't get to you."

"Or maybe the money Mendoza paid them was too good." He drew a breath. "If it hadn't been for Travis, I'd still be there. Maybe not alive, though."

Piper felt cold. "Thank God for Travis. I'm going to be nicer to him from now on." She gathered the French fries and set them outside the tent.

"How nice?"

Piper grinned and kissed a trail down Mark's chest. "Not as nice as I'm going to be to you for the next few minutes."

"IS THERE ANY COFFEE LEFT?" Piper hurried through the door, hoping to breeze through the Dancie-Anna gauntlet. "I'm running late this morning. Anna, when's my first appointment?"

"Now. With Dancie. The website Q&A?"

Right. Drat.

Piper crossed the reception area under Dancie's watchful eye. "You're not twitchy anymore."

"She's not mad anymore, either," Anna added. Helpful Anna.

"Mark and I worked things out." Piper stepped inside Anna's work area and poured coffee into a foam cup. "It was all a big misunderstanding." Deciding to try drinking it black, she escaped to her office.

"You slept with him." Dancie's voice carried clearly.

Piper returned to her doorway and couldn't stop the smile from stretching across her face.

Dancie took one look at her and said, "Anna—"

"Oh, man!" Anna pushed her chair back. "You're going to make me go for croissants, aren't you?"

Without taking her eyes off Piper, Dancie said, "I was going to send you to OMG for some stray résumés that arrived after my brother sent the last batch, but croissants are an excellent idea. Thanks for offering."

"I wasn't exactly— You know he could just email them." Anna looked at the two of them hopefully. "I volunteer to print hard copies."

"I like seeing the originals," Piper said. "Croissants are on me this morning. And I want an almond one. This isn't a chocolate–mocha cream occasion." She sipped her coffee and made a face.

"Get a few of the chocolate ones, too, Anna. It's only a matter of time," Dancie predicted.

The instant a grumbling Anna left, Dancie pounced. "What were you thinking?"

"Thinking is overrated." Piper waved airily. "I think too much. Going with my feelings is a lot more fun."

"What did your feelings do—hijack your brain? Playing with your head wasn't enough? You let him play with your body, too?"

"Mmm." Piper let a tiny smile drift across her face.

"Oh, he's good," Dancie said, shaking her head.

Piper let out a long, slow breath. "Yes, he is."

"Oooookay. Well, now you know. You can take your little Piper Plan quiz and bump up the Mark-like traits on your wish list, and you should be good to go."

"I don't need to take the quiz. He's the one, Dancie." Piper added powdered creamer to her coffee. Marginally better. "All I'd be trying to do is find a man just like him. Why bother when I've got the original?"

Dancie looked at her as though she'd gone nuts. "Because you've only got the original for a few weeks."

"Maybe not."

"That's the afterglow talking. How many women do you think have thought exactly the same thing?"

"This is different."

"Piper." Dancie walked up to her and put a hand on either shoulder. "Look at me. You're trying to find the guy a partner. He is going to leave."

"But I haven't found him a partner yet, have I? And maybe I never will."

"Don't make me shake you."

Piper pulled away. "I doubt I'll find anyone in Travis's leftovers. The ad will have to run again and we'll start the screening process all over. It's already November. Then finals and the holidays. If he's gone by the Super Bowl, I'll be surprised."

"So what's another month?" Dancie asked. "In the end, he's still leaving."

She gave Dancie a smug smile. "By that time, he won't *want* to leave."

"Seriously? Listen to yourself. If you were one of your clients, what would you say?"

"I know it sounds as though I'm deluding myself—"

"Yes! And if I'd thought for a moment that you'd become one of those women who comes in here saying, 'I knew what he was like, but I thought it would be different this time,' I would never have suggested you get involved."

"It *is* different this time." It was. Mark had never connected with a woman the way he had with Piper. He'd told her so, but she'd already known. "Mark isn't going to bounce around the world forever. He's going to want to settle down sometime. Why not with me?"

"You sound exactly like your mother." Dancie clearly thought she'd delivered a killing blow.

"I called my mother," Piper countered.

Dancie's jaw dropped.

Piper savored Dancie's reaction before adding, "And you know what she told me?"

"Heaven only knows."

"She said to follow my heart."

"Of course she did." Dancie leaned back against Piper's desk and crossed her arms. Classic I-don't-want-to-hear-this posture.

Too bad. She was going to hear it. "Mark might be a mistake, but what if he isn't?"

Dancie gazed at her and because Dancie was a true friend, she said, "Okay. Find out. I hope I'm wrong, but if I'm not, I'll be there for you. And I won't say 'I told you so.'"

Piper's phone rang. "Thanks, Dancie."

Dancie nodded and went back to her own desk.

Piper let the phone ring once more while she shifted into professional mode. "Piper Scott."

"Hi. It's Mary Wade. I wanted you to know that after we spoke yesterday, I got a call from Wally Shetland at a regional bureau. Mark had told him about me. We talked, and it looks really good." She gave a surprised laugh. "I'm flying out to Arizona to meet with him, but he said Mark's recommendation was all he needed."

"That's quick!" Mark's thoughtfulness gave her warm fuzzies. "Congratulations. I know Mark thinks you're very talented."

"Thanks. He was right about not leaving my kids. And after the research I've done for him, I can see why."

"Yeah. The Middle East is no picnic for a woman."

"I remember," Mary said. "But I was referring to the Mendoza piece. Mark's got a lot of guts to go back there, but if he didn't take those risks, he wouldn't be Mark Banning."

Go back? "No. He wouldn't." As she spoke, Piper remembered the wall map. The Texas-Mexico border, not the Middle East. The picture of the woman and her sons.

Piper's warm fuzzies turned to icy prickles.

"It would have been a great opportunity and I'd love to help him take down a guy who exploits kids like that, but realistically, it would have been rough on my family for me to leave in a couple of days," Mary said.

"Days? You must have misheard." But Piper knew better. "He's teaching a class this semester."

Mary hesitated and Piper knew her loyalty to a brother journalist was kicking in. "He didn't mention that. He did say that there had been recent developments in the story."

How recent? Piper wondered. Recent since she'd left this morning? Not likely. "Then I guess I'd better check with him because I'm still screening candidates and setting up interviews."

"Good luck finding someone on such short notice," Mary

said with genuine sincerity. "When you get in touch with Mark, would you ask him to call me? I've got some information and a couple of names for him. I only have his office number and he's not answering. I did leave a message, but I want to make sure he gets it."

"I'll tell him. It's very generous of you to keep working under the circumstances."

"Honestly? It feels so good to get my teeth into a meaty story again. He's doing *me* a favor."

Dazzling Mark strikes again.

Piper's first impulse was to call him immediately, but she literally sat on her hands until the feeling passed.

Mark was leaving; she knew that. But he'd planned to leave far sooner than expected and hadn't said anything to her about it. Yeah. There just wasn't a smooth way to say, "By the way, this is a one-night stand." Especially when one of the participants was going on and on about the future and it was obvious she expected you to be a part of it because, of course, what you had together was *special* and this time would be *different.*

Piper had noticed the paperwork spread all over the table and still hadn't registered the significance. Even when telling her about Mendoza, he'd left out the part about a rematch.

Had that Elia woman asked him for help again?

A wave of jealousy swept through her, leaving her shaking.

Mark should have said something to her. Their personal relationship aside— Could she even call it a relationship? She thought not. But they did have a professional relationship and he should have given her a heads-up so she wouldn't waste time testing candidates.

It was tempting to call him and ask for an explanation, but she'd already reacted without hearing his side once. Let him call her. Or at least, Piper was going to do a little digging before she confronted him.

She unplugged her laptop and carried it into the reception area.

Dancie gave no sign that she'd heard anything and honestly, Piper couldn't remember what her half of the conversation had sounded like. "Dancie, do you mind if we postpone working on the website?"

"Yes. But that doesn't mean we can't." She eyed Piper's laptop and scooted her own to one side. "What's up?"

"I want to see what I can find out about the guy who captured Mark." Piper dragged a chair from the waiting area to the desk. "I know OMG has accounts with databases I can't access. I'm hoping you can still get in. Help?"

"Sure. Let me see if my user name and password still work." Dancie went to a web page and logged in. "That one is still good."

Piper looked at the screen. "It's a genealogy site."

"Through which I can access public records. I can find relatives, neighbors, employment records, real estate deeds. Stuff that leads you to other stuff."

"For Mexico?"

"If you know where and how to search. Are you going to tell me what's happening?"

Piper ended up telling her probably more than she wanted to hear.

"You know," Dancie said thoughtfully, "we're forgetting Travis. Those guys he hired to rescue Mark must have a ton of info."

"Mark will have it by now. Can you convince Travis to give us copies without telling Mark?"

"Yes," Dancie answered promptly.

Piper raised an eyebrow and Dancie explained. "He's desperate for help with the Fab Living site, but won't admit it. I'll offer to set up new content for a couple of weeks and he'll agree to anything." She picked up her cell phone. "You know what the best part is? He'll unblock my password rather than go to all the trouble of setting up new accounts for me. And I had an all-access password—which includes the news division."

"Dancie, you are the best friend *ever!*"

"I know," she said.

As Dancie negotiated with Travis, Piper became more and more certain that Mark was about to do something recklessly heroic. He wasn't telling her or anyone else what he planned because he didn't want to be stopped, and he knew any sane person would try to stop him.

When Dancie gave her a thumbs-up, Piper felt weak with relief, even though she didn't know what she'd find or how she'd convince Mark that he was a journalist, and should let the police or some government agency handle Mendoza.

Dancie ended the call, typed on her keyboard and raised her fists in victory. "I'm back!"

"Check out the news division."

"I am, I am." Dancie scrolled through the site map. "Good news, bad news."

"What?"

"I've got access to everything, but I don't know how to use it."

"Mary Wade will. You know, the woman Mark wouldn't take because she has teenagers?"

Dancie nodded.

"I'm calling her." Piper looked up her number. "She's already researching for Mark, anyway."

Within an hour, they'd joined forces with Mary. Anna spoke Spanish, so when she returned from her résumé-and-croissant run, she translated for them.

In the afternoon, Piper had an appointment with the director of a small, private dorm who wanted a questionnaire she could administer to prospective student renters. By the time Piper returned, it was three-thirty, she hadn't heard from Mark, and three grim faces greeted her.

"What?"

"This Mendoza guy is bad news," Dancie said.

"I think we already knew that. Did Mark get in touch with you?" she asked Mary.

Nodding, Mary said, "He got my message. When I offered to keep digging, he said he'd heard from an old contact, so thanks, good luck and all that."

"That sounds like goodbye," Dancie said.

"Yes." Cold settled deep within Piper. "It does sound like goodbye."

MARK WASN'T PROUD that he'd waited until he was actually sitting on the plane before calling Piper, but he knew what she was going to say. Or close enough.

"Hi." Amazing how much meaning could be packed into one little word. Her voice was soft and intimate. A lover's voice.

"Hi." He shut his eyes. This was proving to be harder than he'd expected. "Something has come up and I won't be able to see you tonight."

There was a short silence. "Mendoza?"

His eyes popped open. "Yes."

"Were you going to tell me?"

Damn. "Not if I could avoid it."

"Well, I appreciate your honesty."

Appreciate wasn't *happy* but he'd take it. "I'll be tied up— poor choice of words."

She didn't laugh.

"I'll be busy for the next few days."

"Let me help."

He smiled. "With you around to distract me, we wouldn't get much work done."

"I'm serious," she said. "Mary told me she'd been researching for you. Dancie, Anna and I helped her out this afternoon. You did get her message?"

"Yes. The information was very helpful. Piper, don't take this the wrong way, but I'd rather you didn't involve yourself with this story. Mendoza has a long reach and I don't want anything to happen to you."

"I don't want anything to happen to you, either! Did you call the police? Or the border patrol or whoever's in charge?"

"Yes, I called the appropriate authorities." He hadn't mentioned that he was headed down there, though. "But they're overextended and even if they weren't, they work way too slow. Mendoza always gets tipped off and has plenty of time to move the compound."

"Maybe you just need to give them more information to convince them. I'll come over and show you what we've found."

"I won't be there."

In the seat next to him, the pilot spoke. "We've been cleared for takeoff. You need to wrap that up and put on your headphones."

Mark nodded as Piper's voice sounded loud in his ear. "Are you on a plane?"

"Yes, and I've got to go. I'll call you when I get back."

"Call me when you land."

"Goodbye, Piper." He disconnected the call and pulled the battery from the phone. He would not be calling her when he landed.

Piper watched the call indicator on her cell go dark. She'd stepped outside her office so she wouldn't be overheard. She needn't have bothered. Opening the door, she announced, "Mark's already on a plane. He's on his way to meet with Mendoza."

"By himself?" Mary asked. "That's just—"

"Reckless? Unnecessarily risky? Acting without thinking things through?" Dancie supplied. "In other words, typical Mark."

Anna had gone home and Piper, Dancie and Mary were sharing a pizza.

"Let's go with stupid," Piper said.

"That works, too." Dancie wrapped strings of cheese around a pizza slice.

"But Mark's not stupid," Mary said.

"He's acting stupid." Dancie took a big bite and made a blissful face as she chewed.

"Like ordering vegetarian pizza because you think it's healthy?" Piper asked.

"No, like showing up alone to meet the guy who captured and held you hostage after you humiliated him by escaping."

"Except he wasn't captured. He offered himself in exchange for the boys Mendoza had taken from families in the area."

"That didn't come out in the media coverage." Mary looked concerned. "You don't think he's going to do it again, do you?"

Dancie made a derisive sound. "He's not that stupid."

But he might be that reckless, Piper thought.

"Did he say where's he going?" Mary asked her.

Piper shook her head. "He's on a private plane. I heard the pilot right close by."

"Then we can figure out where he's going—or at least where the plane is going." Mary brushed her hands together and started typing.

"He needs to be careful around Mendoza. This guy is devious and he wants revenge. I don't care what he told Mark." Piper sat by her laptop. "But Mark thinks he knows him." She shook her head. "He doesn't."

Dancie took another piece of pizza. She'd had more than her share, but Piper wasn't all that hungry anymore.

"So are you just going to sit there and wait for him to call? And then you'll tell him all this and he'll say, 'By golly, you're right. I'll turn around and come back to Austin.'"

Piper slumped. Dancie was right.

Dancie put the slice back into the pizza box. "Are y'all finished?"

Both Piper and Mary nodded and waved it away. Dancie closed up the box.

"Where are you going?" Piper asked.

"To Mikey. This is a bribe."

"Half a vegetarian pizza isn't much of a bribe."

Dancie smiled. "I'll make up the other half."

"Who's Mikey and why are you bribing him?" asked Mary.

"A computer guy with mad skills and negotiable ethics," Dancie told her. "And I'm a girl with a golden password."

13

Step thirteen: It's not all about you. Remember that there are two people in your relationship.

"THIS IS MARK BANNING. I was told to call this number when I arrived at La Hermosa Casa. I've arrived." He gazed out his window at the enclosed patio and the pristine fountain. This was a pretty ritzy place to conduct the sort of business they'd be conducting.

But he didn't get to pick the place, or which side of the border it was on. He was still in Texas, but didn't think he would be for long.

A youthful voice spoke. "Senor Mark?"

He didn't quite recognize it, but took a guess. "Gilberto?"

"Yes, you remember."

So Mendoza got him back after all. Mark wasn't surprised.

"I am to tell you to wait for instructions."

"And when will I—" But the call had ended.

Great. Power games. He wouldn't bother to unpack. Instead, Mark took off his shoes and stretched out on the puffy comforter and slept.

"HAS HE FOUND MARK YET?" Piper had pulled into a rest stop off the highway but she didn't plan to rest. But then, had she planned anything before getting in the car and heading south? No. She'd acted. Mark wouldn't answer his phone? Fine, she'd go to him. The fact that she didn't know exactly where he was didn't stop her. Yeah, she was way out of her comfort zone.

Mark was out of her comfort zone.

Piper wasn't sure she even had a comfort zone anymore.

It was the middle of the night and she was in the middle of nowhere, halfway through the eight-hour drive to Presidio, Texas. She was driving because Presidio was also in the middle of nowhere and the nearest airport to it was four hours away, unless you chartered a plane. Which Mark had. Piper could not afford to charter a plane, so she had to drive. And she had to drive because Mark would not answer her calls. His phone wasn't even on.

She'd been told that the land, near Big Bend State Park, was starkly beautiful. Too bad she couldn't see it in the dark.

"Mikey is at the delicate stage," Dancie murmured into the phone.

"Is that like the tricky stage he was in last time I called, or the difficult stage he was in earlier?"

"This is the better-not-get-caught stage."

"Let's hope he gets to the I-found-him stage by the time I get to Presidio."

MARK HAD RECEIVED two more calls from Gilberto, each coming from a different number. They were obviously using cheap, prepaid cell phones and he couldn't call them back. Gilberto wouldn't answer his questions or talk with him, either, and Mark suspected Mendoza was standing next to him. This was probably a loyalty test for Gilberto, poor kid.

The first instructions had sent Mark to a man whose eyes got wide and face drained of color as soon as he'd opened his door. Then he'd slammed the door. Then there had been a lot a yelling from behind the door, at which point Mark stepped back from the door. It opened and a young boy gave him a set of keys and pointed to an ancient, faded red pickup truck parked in the dirt driveway. Then he held out his hand and pointed to Mark's silver, midsize rental.

Mark dropped the key into the boy's palm. "That's gonna put a hole in the budget."

Without responding, the boy went back inside. Mark had his doubts about the pickup, but it started right up and shifted smoothly into gear. He gave it a little gas and it responded with a deep rumble. Okay. Junker on the outside, hidden power on the inside. Like Mendoza.

Mark drove it back to La Hermosa Casa and shortly after, the second call instructed him to open a bank account. He'd just returned from that chore. He figured Mendoza was watching him to see if anyone was with him. When he was satisfied, he'd contact Mark with meeting instructions.

A little later, when Mark heard someone knock on the door, he thought maybe Mendoza had sent an escort to the meeting site. He hoped it was Gilberto, although Mendoza was unlikely to send the boy across the border alone.

Steeling himself, Mark opened the door and was met with angry brown eyes. Déjà vu.

He blinked. "Piper?" She was here? Stunned, he stood aside. "How did you find me?"

"Dancie's boyfriend has mad skills." She rolled a suitcase across the room to the desk.

"Obviously illegal skills."

"He used a difficult, tricky, delicate procedure." Piper opened the suitcase and removed her laptop and assorted papers. "And vegetarian pizza was involved. That's all I know."

Mark was so astounded that she was here, so thrown off balance, that he spent several minutes caught up in watching her and trying to figure out how she'd managed it.

The desk phone rang and snapped him out of it. The timing was horrible. He couldn't deal with Mendoza *and* Piper simultaneously.

"Shall I answer?" She reached for the phone.

"No!" As he leapt forward, she snatched her hand back.

"Is that Mendoza?"

"I don't know. Let me focus." He paused, trying to block out the image of the woman standing next to him, and picked up the phone. "Banning."

"He wants to meet." It was Gilberto again.

"He hasn't told me what he wants from me yet."

"Three hours from now." Gilberto started giving GPS coordinates.

Mark grabbed for the pen, but Piper had moved everything on the desk. "Gilberto, wait—I need to write this down." He shoved her papers roughly, but couldn't find anything to write with.

Silently, she handed him a pen and he wrote on the nearest paper he found. Gilberto hadn't paused reciting the numbers and Mark quickly wrote what he remembered and caught up with the rest. "I need to verify that. I've got—"

The phone went dead. Instantly, he tried to call back, but the call had come through the hotel switchboard and he knew Gilberto would have immediately tossed the phone.

Mark stared at the scribbled coordinates. "I don't even know which side of the border this is on. And I'm not sure I even wrote them down right." He glared at a still-silent Piper. "This is why I work alone. I get distracted when I should focus. What if I made a mistake and don't show up at the right place?"

"I say 'yay' because you shouldn't be going, anyway." She plucked the paper from his grasp.

"That's not your decision."

Standing, her laptop open, Piper typed the coordinates into a map program. She turned the computer around to face him. "Does this look right?"

He looked at a remote area near the border on the U.S.

side. "Maybe." He turned his attention to her. "You shouldn't be here."

"Neither should you."

"This is my job. This is who I am. This is what I do."

She was shaking her head, golden-brown hair brushing her shoulders. "You're not writing a story—you're on a rescue mission."

He remembered the way her hair felt brushing his skin, the way she felt—but he shouldn't be remembering; he needed to think and prepare for this upcoming meeting. "Piper, I know we..."

"Had a thing together that meant more to me than it did to you? Just because we had sex doesn't mean I have the right to tell you what to do or how to do it? This part of your life has nothing to do with me and I should stay out of it? Does that about sum it up?" Piper's unemotional mask was back in place and her eyes were blank. Almost.

"Yes," he said.

She didn't flinch.

"When I'm working, I need to make instant decisions and I can't second-guess myself. I can't stop and wonder whether you think what I'm doing is dangerous or risky or wrong." He gestured to the paper where he'd written the meeting location. "You've only been here five minutes and I may have already blown it."

"I can accept dangerous and risky, but not wrong." She began searching through the papers he'd mixed up.

He squeezed his eyes shut. "I can't do this. I can't."

"You promised."

Mark started to deny he'd ever make a promise like that. "I—"

"You promised you would listen to my opinion," she interrupted. "You don't have to agree, but you have to truly consider it."

He remembered. "That was about finding my partner."

"If you won't listen to someone who just drove all night to bring you information you need, you'll never work with anyone."

"I never wanted to work with anyone."

"Too bad. Now pay attention."

Arguing would only waste more time. "Okay."

"I heard you say 'Gilberto.'" She placed printouts on the desk.

"He's my contact."

"Gilberto from the photo?"

He nodded and she pointed to a picture on one of the printouts. "This Gilberto?"

Mark studied the group. It was a recent multigenerational family photo surrounding a bride and groom. The bride was Elia. He didn't recognize the groom. Other than being glad she'd found happiness, he felt nothing for her. He picked out Gilberto, who'd grown, and Hector, who still looked boyish, standing next to their mother. Behind them stood Mendoza. "So?"

"You do see Mendoza?"

"She probably married one of his people. Or it's been Photoshopped."

"She's his sister, Mark. He's their uncle."

Mark laughed. "You drove all night to tell me that?"

"You already knew?"

"Oh, Piper." Still chuckling, he drew her to him. "He's not their uncle."

Briefly, she relaxed against him before pushing away. "Yes, he is. I've found documentation to prove it."

Mark shook his head. "I've spent almost two years of my life collecting information about Mendoza. I wouldn't have missed that. And even if I had, I stayed with Elia and the boys. I saw how frantic she was. Do you really think she wouldn't have told me?"

Piper's face softened. "You were set up. You were poking around, threatening him and he took you out."

"A bullet to the head would have been a lot less trouble."

She held up a finger. "But that's not the way his type operates."

Oh, no. Not the grid squares.

"He needs to show both power and cleverness," Piper said. "When that team came in and rescued you, you humiliated him. I don't know what he's told you, but trust me, this is all about revenge. He'll destroy the thing you value most in a way that demonstrates his power."

"Give me some credit. This is just a meeting. He wants something—probably weapons—in exchange for Hector and some other boys. So if he's going to make his move, it'll be when I'm delivering whatever it is he wants. Today, all he's going to do is parade the boys in front of me so I can see how scared they are. It's a negotiating ploy to jack up the price." It would be unpleasant, but Mark knew he wasn't in any personal danger yet.

Piper looked down at the desk. "I've got all kinds of information here, but I know you won't read it. So I'll say this." When she looked back at him, she'd dropped the mask and her eyes were full of emotion. "Unless those boys are what you value most in your life, that's not what's at stake."

She cared about him and she believed what she said.

"It means a lot that you came all this way," he told her. "But I can't just forget about them. I promised I'd help."

She took a step forward. "You don't have to do it alone!"

This was about to become just the kind of teary scene he avoided. "Piper, you're overthinking this." He grabbed his GPS and programmed in the coordinates. "I've got to go. This has taken way too much time."

He was grateful when she didn't say anything else, but still, he avoided looking at her as he collected a satchel, sunglasses, and shrugged into his jacket. She walked with him to the door.

They stared at each other. "I'll be fine," he told her.

But Piper planted her hands on either side of his face and kissed him fiercely. "I'll never forget you, Mark Banning."

Piper had given it her best shot. She'd hoped Mark would look at the material she and Mary and Dancie had collected, but he hadn't. At least she'd given him the two most important pieces of information. It was hard to let him walk out without begging him to stay or going after him, but it was his decision.

It would be a whole lot easier to accept it if she wasn't in love with him. She should have told him. She'd meant to, but at the last moment, she'd heard herself saying she'd never forget him. And it was true, but it was the type of thing people said when they never expected to see each other again.

And that was probably why she'd said it.

HER PARTING WORDS ECHOED in his mind, no matter how much he tried to ignore them.

Mark drove as fast as he could on the open highway, trying to make up for the late start and the fact that he'd soon have to turn onto unpaved roads. There was very little traffic and once the GPS alerted him to the turnoff, there was nothing to break the monotony of miles of scrubby landscape.

He checked the gas gauge, something he should have done before starting out. And he would have, if Piper hadn't distracted him. Lucky for him, there was plenty of gas.

Piper. *I'll never forget you.*

She'd driven all the way to Presidio to tell him Mendoza was the boys' uncle. Honorary uncle, at the most. And probably forced.

But she was right about the guy being clever. Using Gilberto as a go-between was deliberate. A little dig. Gilberto had been Mark's best source of information about how Mendoza used the network of boys, and Mark hated knowing he must have been punished for talking with him. No one else would say much of anything, out of fear. The families rarely, if ever, saw their sons again. Mark knew from the time he spent at the main compound that Mendoza offered visits home as rewards. But had any boy ever earned one?

Mark's foot eased on the accelerator.

You were set up.

He's their uncle.

No. He pressed the gas again. Thanks to Piper, he was second-guessing himself. This was exactly why he worked alone.

But how had Gilberto been able to talk with his friends if he never saw them?

For the next few miles, Mark's thoughts churned until the GPS signaled that he was approaching the turnoff. Mark slowed until he was right beside it, but instead of turning, he stopped.

Where was he headed? There was nothing around him and this turn took him away from the mountains he assumed were his destination. The next section of the route took him close to the border where he was bound to encounter patrols. Not that he had anything to hide, but he'd rather stay under the radar, since he wasn't officially on assignment.

And Mendoza knew it.

He'll destroy the thing you value most.

I'll never forget you.

She would *not* get out of his head.

Or his heart, either.

Mark bashed his hands against the steering wheel and stared at the road. Then he turned the truck around and drove back to the hotel.

HOURS BEFORE PIPER EXPECTED him to return, she heard a card key in the lock and an instant later, an angry Mark stalked over to where she worked at the desk. "Mark, you scared me! What happened?"

He glared at her. "I love you, that's what happened!" Exhaling, he paced over to the window and stared out, his back to her.

He'd said *love,* right? But he hadn't said it like it was a good thing. Piper watched the rise and fall of his shoulders. "Did you meet with Mendoza?"

"No, I didn't meet with Mendoza!" He turned around and paced back over to her. "How could I meet with Mendoza when your voice wouldn't get out of my head?"

Piper decided it was a rhetorical question.

He closed his eyes and rubbed the bridge of his nose before telling her what happened. "I kept thinking about what you said. I began to question everything, second-guessing myself. I *hate* that."

"I know," she said quietly.

"You said you'd never forget me."

"I won't."

"That's my thing." He paced around her as he talked. "I was determined to leave a journalistic legacy so great that no one would ever forget me. I thought being forgotten as though I'd never existed was the worst thing that could ever happen to me." He came to a stop in front of her. "You know what's worse?"

Piper shook her head.

"Being remembered for the wrong thing, for doing something bad."

"Your reputation. Of course." She knew she was right. "Mendoza wants to destroy your reputation because that's what you value most."

"But it isn't." Mark drew her out of the chair and into his arms. "You are." And he kissed her with all the romance and passion lacking in his earlier angry statement.

Piper stopped thinking and let herself absorb all the emotions in that kiss. It had cost him to acknowledge his feelings and make himself vulnerable. Piper vowed he'd never regret it.

Eventually, they came up for air and Mark rested his forehead against hers. "Now what?"

"Well," Piper said. "There's the bed, or we can catch Mendoza. Your choice."

Mark narrowed his eyes. "Is that a trick or some sort of test?"

Piper shook her head. "The truth is that I am exhausted. I was up all night and I've been worried about you for a long time. Now that you're safe, I feel myself crashing."

"We're not safe." His face was grim and he'd included her.

"So we'll get rid of Mendoza." Piper led him over to the desk. "Here's what we found. Take a look at it and if you have questions, contact Dancie and Mary. By the way, I had Travis hire Mary as your temporary research assistant so your trip here is on the books. Just in case you needed rescuing and BT needed persuading."

He looked sheepish. "Thanks."

"By the way, did you open a bank account?"

"Yes," he admitted slowly. "How did you know? Dancie's boyfriend?"

"Don't ask."

"Not asking."

Piper gripped the back of her neck and looked at him uncertainly. "Don't get mad, but you need to work with the authorities on this."

"I've tried. They're not interested." Mark stepped behind her and began rubbing her shoulders. It felt so good, she could fall asleep standing up.

"Weeeell, you'll probably find them more interested now."

His hands fingers. "What have you—"

Piper held up a hand.

"I don't need to know," Mark said. "Do I owe Dancie's boyfriend a pizza?"

"Several pizzas," Piper told him. "Even more after we catch Mendoza." She yawned and he nudged her toward the bed. "Promise you won't catch him while I'm asleep?"

Mark smiled down at her. "Promise."

FOUR DAYS AND A DOZEN pizzas later, Mendoza and his men were in custody, and the boys had been returned to their families.

The red pickup truck had been specially modified to smuggle illicit cargo. Between that and the bank account, and other surprises Mendoza had put into place, Mark would have been involved in a messy scandal at the least and likely would have ended up in prison.

They had their first argument over how many times Piper was entitled to say "I told you so."

"Piper?"

Piper had been packing and trying to pretend she wanted to leave. The truth was that the past few days had been thrilling, and exciting, and tense, and fulfilling and she didn't want to go back. Dancie could have the office. Dancie could have everything.

Except Mark. Mark would be in Austin for a few more weeks, but after that...

Pasting on a fake smile, she looked up to find Mark regarding her with a troubled expression. Uh-oh. "What?"

"I don't know how to do this."

Alarm filled her. "How to do what?"

"Have a relationship." He swallowed. "I don't know how it's supposed to work, but I do know we can't have one if we're not together."

He was breaking up with her. Piper's heart squeezed and she couldn't breathe. She didn't want to breathe. Maybe she'd pass out and wouldn't have to hear what he said next.

"I know it's asking a lot, but I want you to come with me. Be my researcher. Do the same thing you've been doing the last few days—except without the help of Dancie's boyfriend."

She gasped and became a little light-headed. "You're asking me to go overseas with you? To work as your partner?" They'd made a great team, but she didn't think he'd even consider it.

Mark nodded. "You always said you could find me the right person."

"I did." She grinned. "But you're sure you don't need someone with more experience?"

"I need you. Besides, you're good at it." He looped his arms around her. "You're good for me."

Piper beamed at him. "I am *great* for you. I am *perfect* for you."

"I love you." His mouth quirked. "I don't want to mess this up."

"I love you, too. And I am not going to *let* you mess this up."

Epilogue

Congratulations on completing THE PIPER PLAN and landing your perfect man! We at Perfectly Fabulous Plans, LLC, hope he agrees that you're his perfect woman and you're having a fabulous life together. If you'd like further help, please check out HOW TO KEEP IT FABULOUS: Living with Your Perfect Man, and COMMITTING: How to Take the Next Step.

A year later.

"I MISS THE WIG." Mark propped an elbow on the counter and tweaked a lock of Piper's shoulder-length hair.

"I've missed the fries." She inhaled Friezen Burger's grease-laden air. "Toni's still here. Do you think she'll remember me?"

"You are unforgettable," Mark told her, and sent a lazy smile down the bar where Toni was taking an order.

Sure enough, within moments, Toni raised her head, lit up in recognition and headed toward them.

"Clearly, so are you," Piper said. She'd accepted that all over the world, women just loved Mark. She couldn't blame them, because so did she.

Toni leaned on the counter, eyes only for Mark. "Long time no see."

"We've been out of the country or nothing would have kept us away from your fries." He slipped an arm around Piper's waist.

Toni's gaze shifted.

"Hi, Toni.

Toni blinked.

"It's Piper. No wig today."

"Oh! Hey." She looked at the two of them. "Welcome back. What can I get you?"

"One classic basket and a long platter," Mark said.

Toni made a note. "Any sauces to go with that?"

He looked down at Piper and his eyes darkened. "Maybe later."

A look. *That* look was all it took, even after a year together, to send the familiar molten feeling spreading through her body and cause her heart to beat with heavy, syrupy thuds.

They'd seen each other at their best and their worst, impatient and irritated (Mark) and anxious and stubborn (Piper).

And this past year had been the best of her life.

A year ago, she'd thought she wanted security and stability and a man with whom she could put down roots so deep, no one could ever rip them out.

With Mark, every day had been different. They'd had adventures, both good and bad, and the only constant in her life had been Mark. And that was exactly the way she wanted it.

MARK HADN'T MEANT TO keep Piper away from Austin for an entire year, but the longer they were away, the more he dreaded returning.

What if she never wanted to leave again?

Then he wouldn't, either.

He'd always known having a long-term relationship would mean the end of his lengthy and risky assignments. What he hadn't anticipated was that he wouldn't mind. Having her with him this past year had absolutely affected his work. It was better, richer. He hadn't seen that coming at all. Heck, even Dancie and her friend Mikey had moved in together, making a family with Chip and Lexie from the shelter. If they could do it, so could he.

But, now, it was Piper's turn to make the plans, and Mark was going to make sure they included him.

Their order arrived and Piper snatched one of the fries before Toni finished setting the basket in front of them.

"Mmm." She chewed with her eyes closed. "I have *really* missed these."

"They're the best," Mark agreed.

"And we know that because we ate French fries everywhere we went and they weren't even close to these." Piper took a few more and tried not to gobble them. She savored the earthy saltiness, the crunch and the fluffy potato inside. They were good, even when cold, but they were great when hot.

"Hey, you're not eating."

Mark had put some on the platter. "At the rate you're inhaling those, I was afraid I might not have enough."

"You can always order more. You know, if you leave them in the basket, they won't cool off so fast."

"I know." He pinched one in half and curved the two pieces. "But they're easier to shape when they're cooler."

"What?" And then Piper saw that the two curved pieces became part of two *R*s.

Mark had spelled out *MARRY ME* with fries. As Piper struggled to swallow, he twisted a last fry into a question mark and nudged a stray bit into place for the dot.

A question, not a demand.

A year ago, Piper would have thought about it and asked what his plans were, where he saw them living, about children and finances and how to split domestic chores before giving her answer.

But that was last year.

Now, she ate an *M,* scooted the *Y* and the *E* together, raided the *R*s for the curves to make an *S,* and straightened the question mark into an exclamation point.

Pretty good for someone whose hands were shaking.

She looked up to find that incredibly charming dazzler of women, Mark Banning, with his eyes closed, exhaling in relief. How had he thought she'd say anything other than "yes"?

"I—"

"—Love you."

They'd spoken at the same time. "So much," Piper added, "that sometimes—"

"It hurts to breathe," Mark finished.

It was exactly what she'd been going to say.

Toni stopped by. "Can I get you two anything else?"

Mark gave Piper a blazing hot look with a smile that dazzled her into forgetting the rest of the world existed.

Just as her jaw went slack, she heard, "Toni, would you wrap these fries up to go?"

* * * * *

COMING NEXT MONTH from Harlequin® Blaze™
AVAILABLE JULY 24, 2012

#699 FEELS LIKE HOME
Sons of Chance
Vicki Lewis Thompson
Rafe Locke has come to the Last Chance Ranch for his brother's wedding, but he's not happy about it. After all, Rafe is a city slicker, through and through—until sexy Meg Seymour *shows* him all the advantages of going country....

#700 BLAZING BEDTIME STORIES, VOLUME VIII
Kimberly Raye and Julie Leto
Join bestselling authors Kimberly Raye and Julie Leto as they take you to Neverland—that is, *Texas*—in these two sizzling stories, guaranteed to make you want to do anything but sleep.

#701 BAREFOOT BLUE JEAN NIGHT
Made in Montana
Debbi Rawlins
Travel blogger Jamie Daniels is determined to show sexy cowboy Cole McAllister that she's not like all the other girls—in and out of bed.

#702 THE MIGHTY QUINNS: DERMOT
The Mighty Quinns
Kate Hoffmann
With just a bus ticket and $100 in his pocket, Dermot Quinn sets out to experience life as his immigrant grandfather had—penniless and living in unfamiliar surroundings. So the last thing he expects is to strike it rich with country girl Rachel Howe.

#703 GUILTY PLEASURES
Tori Carrington
Former Army Ranger turned security expert Jonathon Reece always gets the job done. This time, his assignment is to bring in fugitive-from-justice Mara Findlay. Too bad the sexy bad girl outwits him at every turn...including in bed.

#704 LIGHT ME UP
Friends with Benefits
Isabel Sharpe
Imagine walking into a photography studio run by the sexiest man you've ever seen and finding pictures...all of you. Jack Shea has captured her essence, but is Melissa Weber ready to bare even more?

REQUEST YOUR FREE BOOKS!
2 FREE NOVELS PLUS 2 FREE GIFTS!

♦Harlequin®
Blaze™

red-hot reads!

YES! Please send me 2 FREE Harlequin® Blaze™ novels and my 2 FREE gifts (gifts are worth about $10). After receiving them, if I don't wish to receive any more books, I can return the shipping statement marked "cancel." If I don't cancel, I will receive 6 brand-new novels every month and be billed just $4.49 per book in the U.S. or $4.96 per book in Canada. That's a saving of at least 14% off the cover price. It's quite a bargain. Shipping and handling is just 50¢ per book in the U.S. and 75¢ per book in Canada.* I understand that accepting the 2 free books and gifts places me under no obligation to buy anything. I can always return a shipment and cancel at any time. Even if I never buy another book, the two free books and gifts are mine to keep forever.

151/351 HDN FEQE

Name _____ (PLEASE PRINT)

Address _____ Apt. #

City _____ State/Prov. _____ Zip/Postal Code

Signature (if under 18, a parent or guardian must sign)

Mail to the **Reader Service:**
IN U.S.A.: P.O. Box 1867, Buffalo, NY 14240-1867
IN CANADA: P.O. Box 609, Fort Erie, Ontario L2A 5X3

Not valid for current subscribers to Harlequin Blaze books.

Want to try two free books from another line?
Call 1-800-873-8635 or visit www.ReaderService.com.

* Terms and prices subject to change without notice. Prices do not include applicable taxes. Sales tax applicable in N.Y. Canadian residents will be charged applicable taxes. Offer not valid in Quebec. This offer is limited to one order per household. All orders subject to credit approval. Credit or debit balances in a customer's account(s) may be offset by any other outstanding balance owed by or to the customer. Please allow 4 to 6 weeks for delivery. Offer available while quantities last.

Your Privacy—The Reader Service is committed to protecting your privacy. Our Privacy Policy is available online at www.ReaderService.com or upon request from the Reader Service.

We make a portion of our mailing list available to reputable third parties that offer products we believe may interest you. If you prefer that we not exchange your name with third parties, or if you wish to clarify or modify your communication preferences, please visit us at www.ReaderService.com/consumerschoice or write to us at Reader Service Preference Service, P.O. Box 9062, Buffalo, NY 14269. Include your complete name and address.

HB11B

*Montana. Home of big blue skies, wide open spaces…and
really hot men! Join bestselling author Debbi Rawlins in
celebrating all things Western in Harlequin® Blaze™
with her new miniseries, MADE IN MONTANA!*

Read on for a sneak peek of
BAREFOOT BLUE JEAN NIGHT

"OVER HERE," Cole said.

Jamie headed toward him, her lips rising in a cheeky
grin. "What makes you think I'm looking for you?"

He drew her back into the shadows inside the barn.
"Then tell me, Jamie, what are you looking for?"

A spark had ignited between them and she had the
distinct feeling that tonight was the night for fireworks—
despite the threat of thieves. The only unanswered question
was when.

"Oh, I get it," she said finally. "You're trying to distract
me from telling you I'm going to help you keep watch."

He lowered both hands. "No, you're not."

"I am. Rachel thinks it's an excellent idea."

He shot a frown toward the kitchen. "I don't care what
my sister thinks. You have five minutes, then you're marching right back into that house."

She wasn't about to let him get away with pulling back.
Not to mention she didn't care for his bossiness. "You're
such a coward."

"Let's put it this way…" He arched a brow. "How much
watching do you think we'd get done?"

She flattened a palm on his chest. His heart pounded as
hard as hers. "I see your point. But no, I won't be a good
little girl and do as you so charmingly ordered."

"It wasn't an order," he muttered. "It was a strongly

worded request. I have to stay alert out here."

"Correct. That's why we'll behave like adults and refrain from making out."

"Making out," he repeated with a snort. "Haven't heard that term in a while." Then he caught her wrist and pulled her hand away from his chest. "Not a good start."

"It's barely dark. No one's going to sneak in now. Once we seriously need to pay attention, I'll be as good as gold. But I figure we have at least an hour."

"For?"

"Oh, I don't know…" With the tip of her finger she traced his lower lip. "Nothing too risky. Just some kissing. Maybe I'll even let you get to first base."

Cole laughed. "Honey, I've never stopped at first base before and I'm not about to start now."

Don't miss BAREFOOT BLUE JEAN NIGHT
by Debbi Rawlins.

Available August 2012 from Harlequin® Blaze™
wherever books are sold.

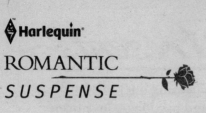

❤ Harlequin®

ROMANTIC
SUSPENSE

CINDY DEES

takes you on a wild journey to find the truth
in her new miniseries

Code X

Aiden McKay is more than just an ordinary man. As part of
an elite secret organization, Aiden was genetically enhanced
to increase his lung capacity and spend extended time under
water. He is a committed soldier, focused and dedicated
to his job. But when Aiden saves impulsive free spirit
Sunny Jordan from drowning she promptly overturns his
entire orderly, solitary world.

As the danger creeps closer, Adien soon realizes Sunny is the
target…but can he save her in time?

Breathless Encounter

Find out this August!

Look out for a reader-favorite bonus story included in each
Harlequin Romantic Suspense book this August!